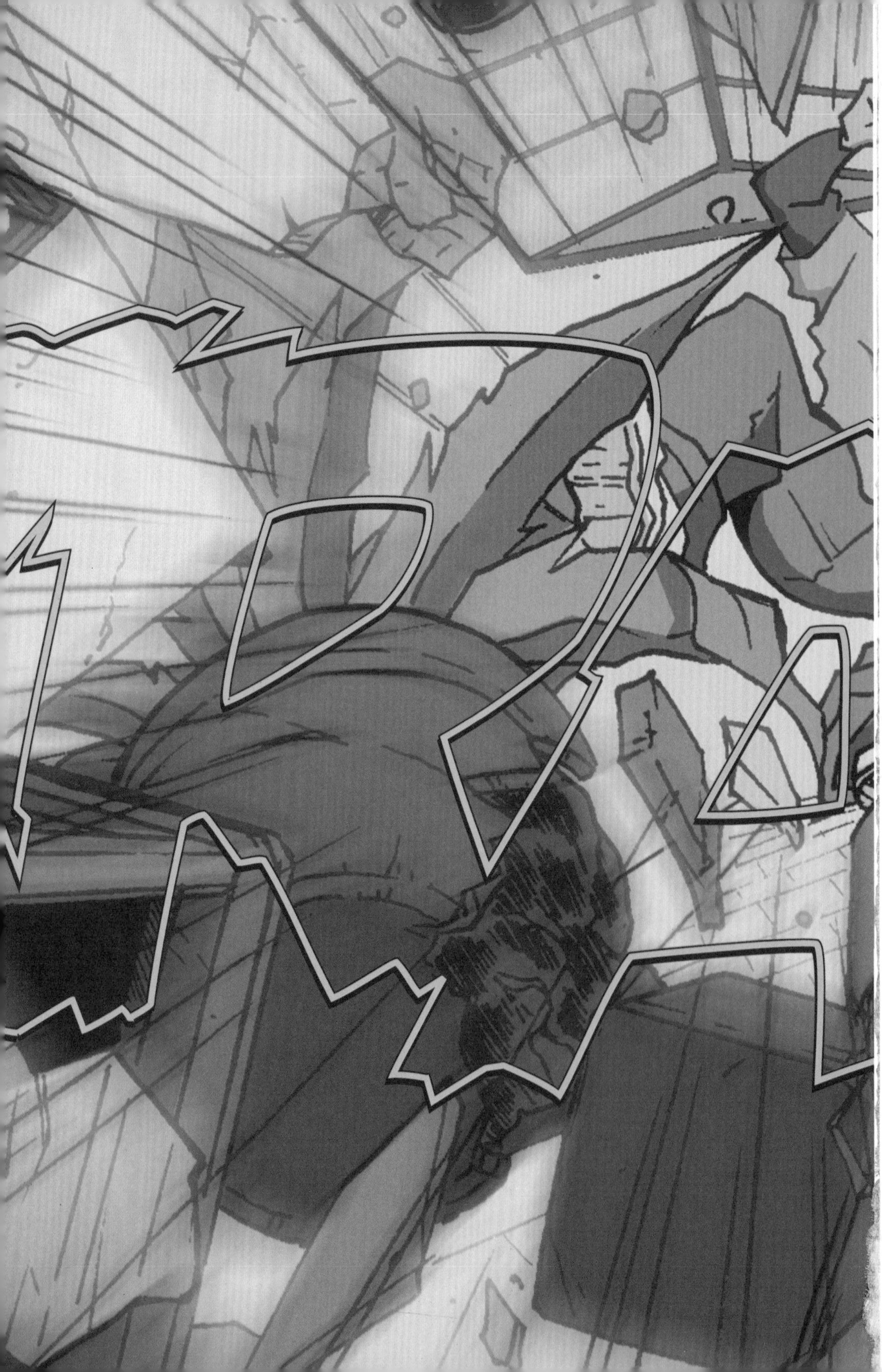

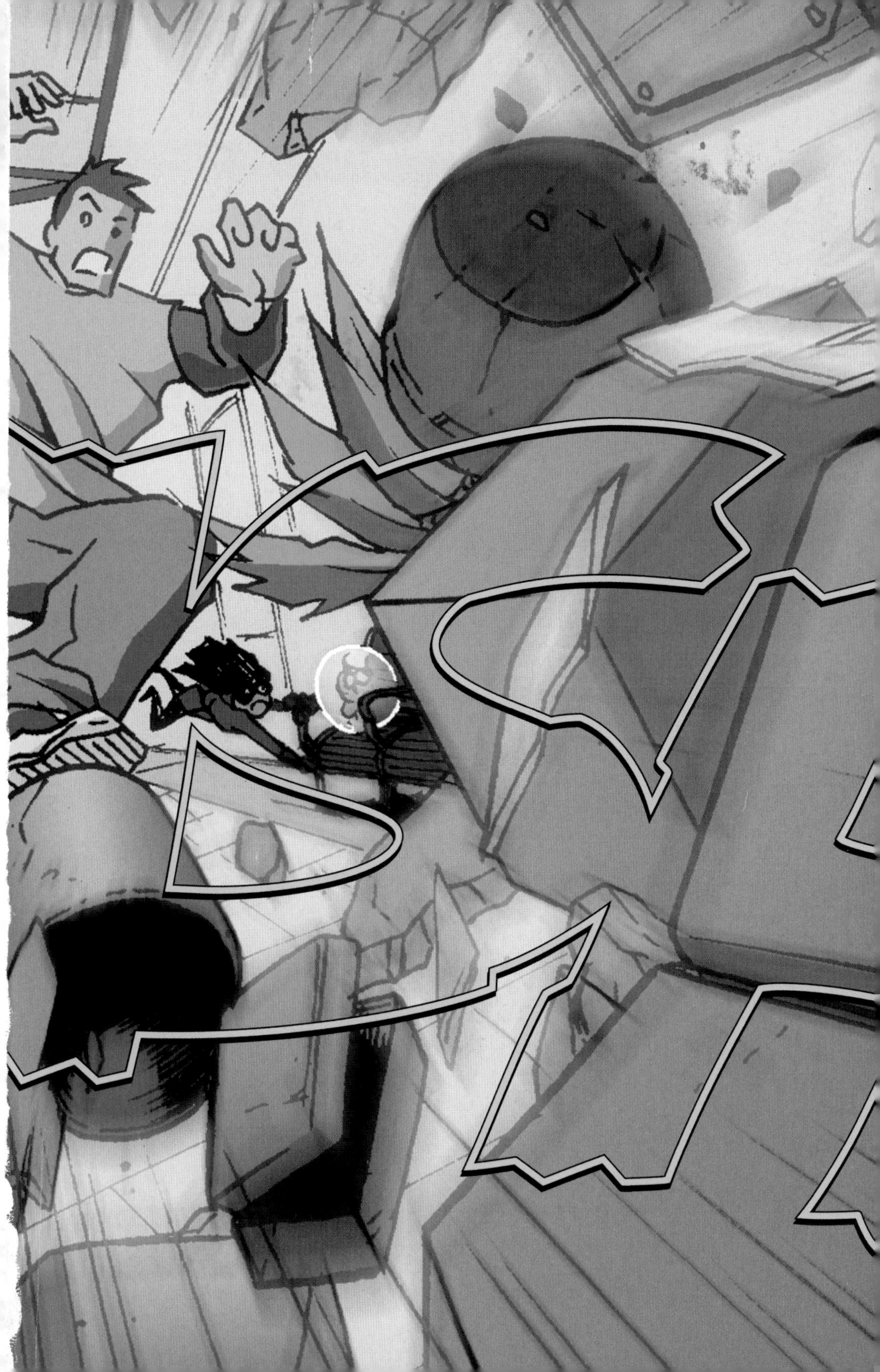

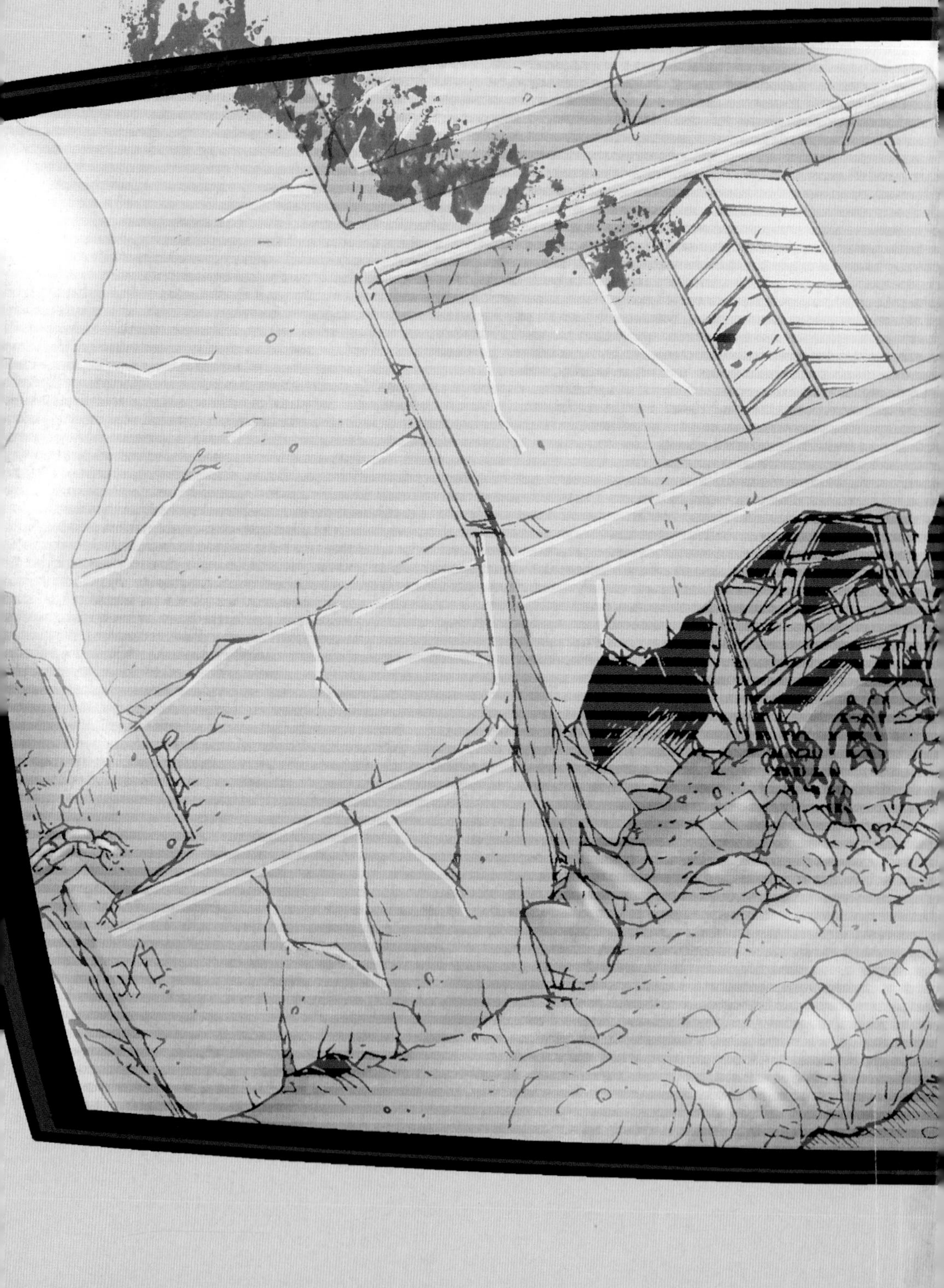

Disney · PIXAR

THE INCREDIBLES

CITY OF INCREDIBLES

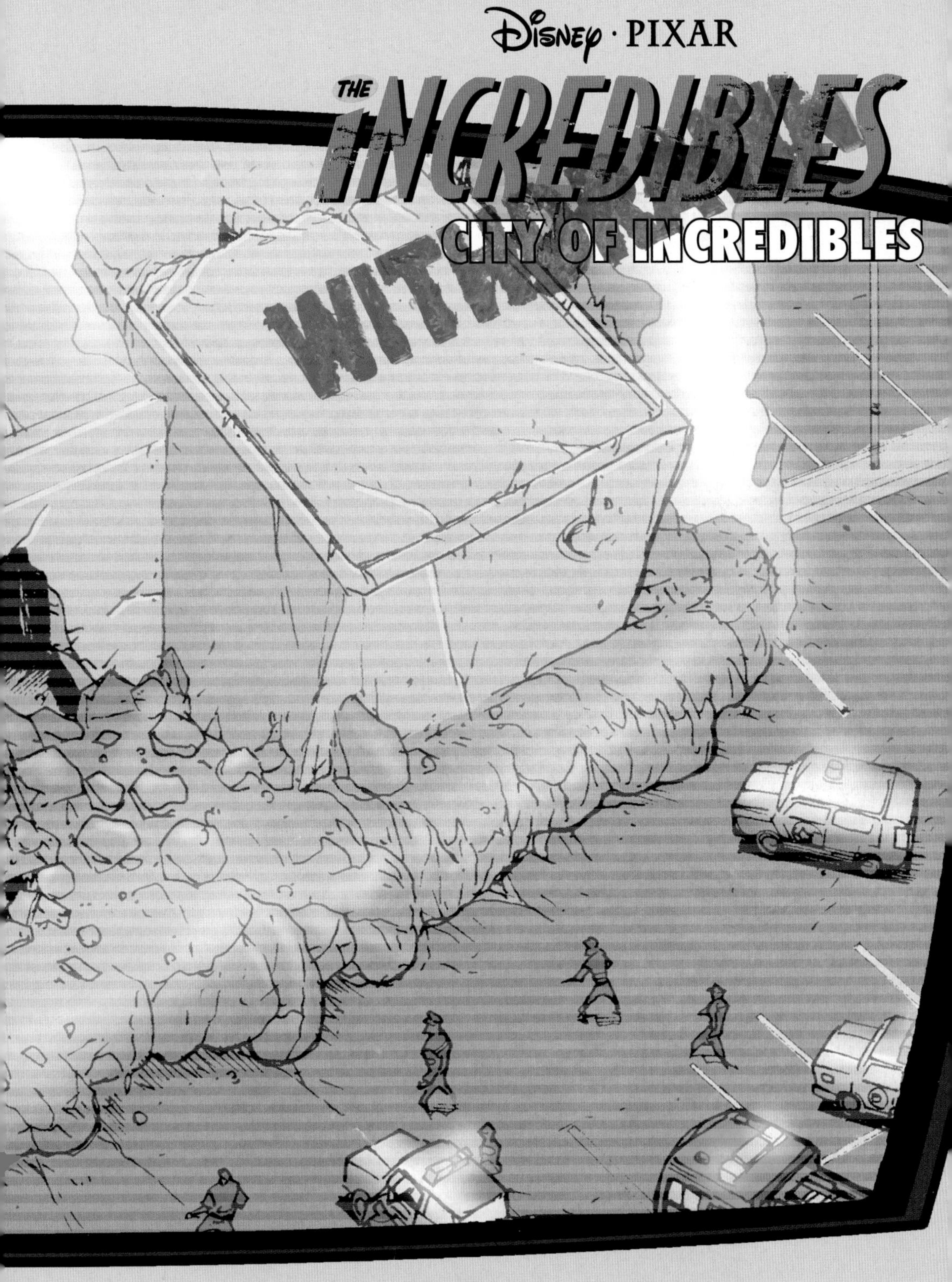

Disney · PIXAR

THE INCREDIBLES

CITY OF INCREDIBLES

ROSS RICHIE
chief executive officer

MARK WAID
editor-in-chief

ADAM FORTIER
vice president,
publishing

CHIP MOSHER
marketing director

MATT GAGNON
managing editor

JENNY CHRISTOPHER
sales director

FIRST EDITION: DECEMBER 2009

10 9 8 7 6 5 4 3 2 1
PRINTED BY WORLD COLOR PRESS, INC.,
ST-ROMUALD, QC., CANADA.

Office of publication: 6310 San Vicente Blvd Ste 404, Los Angeles, CA 90048.

A catalog record for this book is available from the Library of Congress and on our website at

WRITERS:
MARK WAID
PROLOGUE

MARK WAID AND LANDRY WALKER
CHAPTERS 1-3

ART BY:

MARCIO TAKARA AND RAMANDA KAMARGA
PROLOGUE & CHAPTER 2   CHAPTERS 1 &3

COLORS: ANDREW DALHOUSE
LETTERS: TROY PETERI

DESIGNER: ERIKA TERRIQUEZ
EDITOR: AARON SPARROW

COVER ARTIST: MARCIO TAKARA
COLORS BY: ANDREW DALHOUSE

PROLOGUE

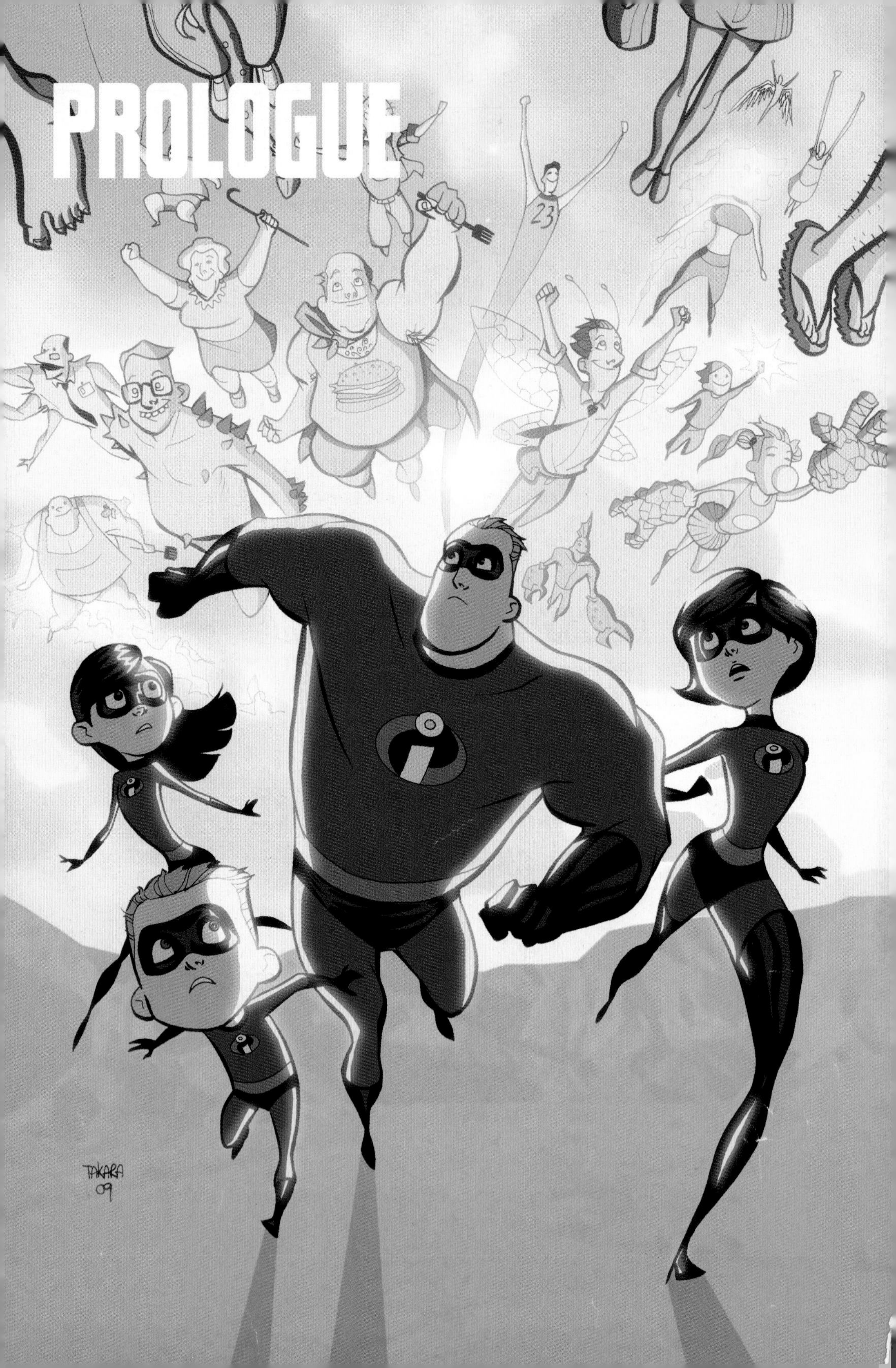
23
TAKARA
09

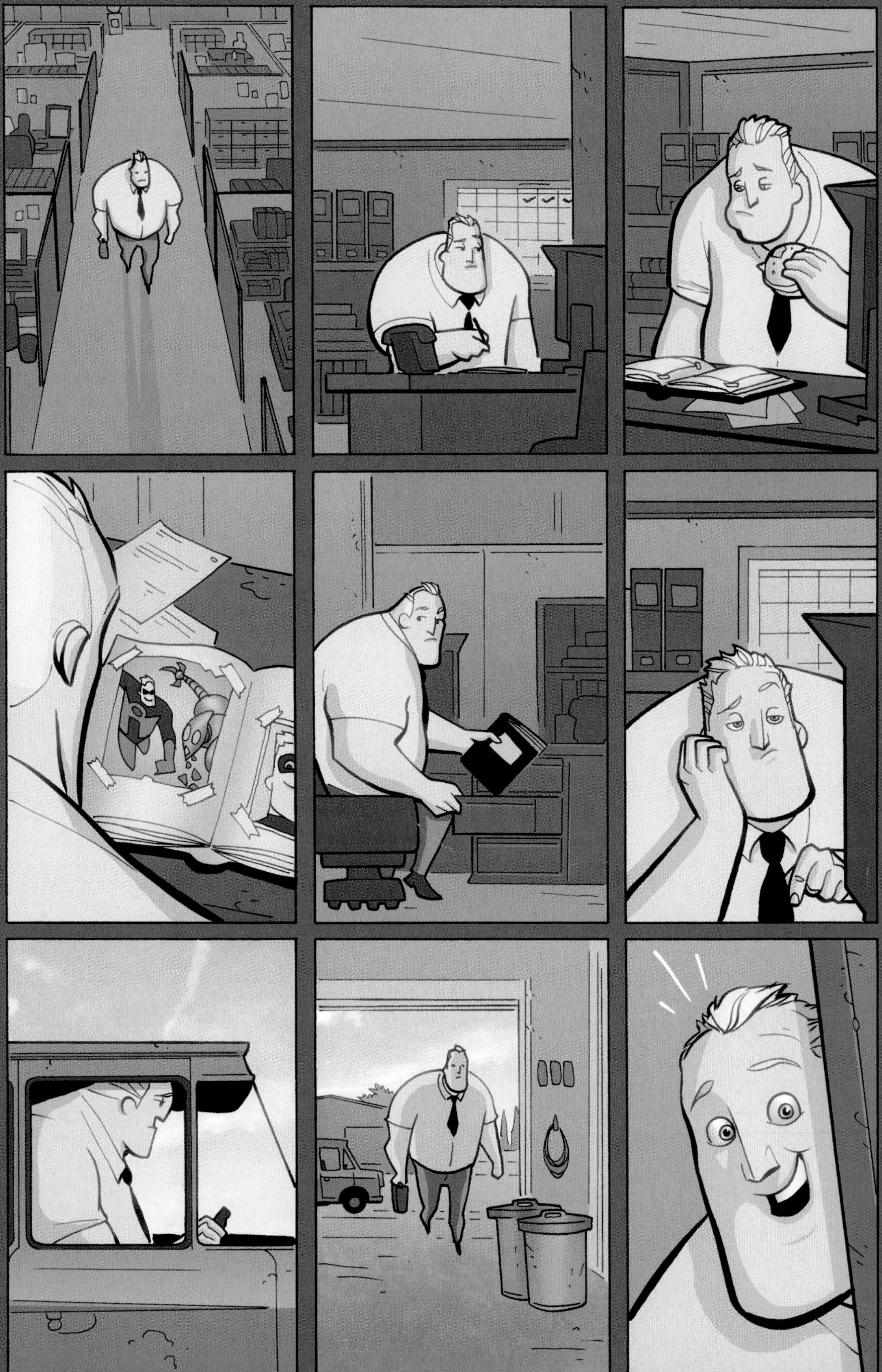

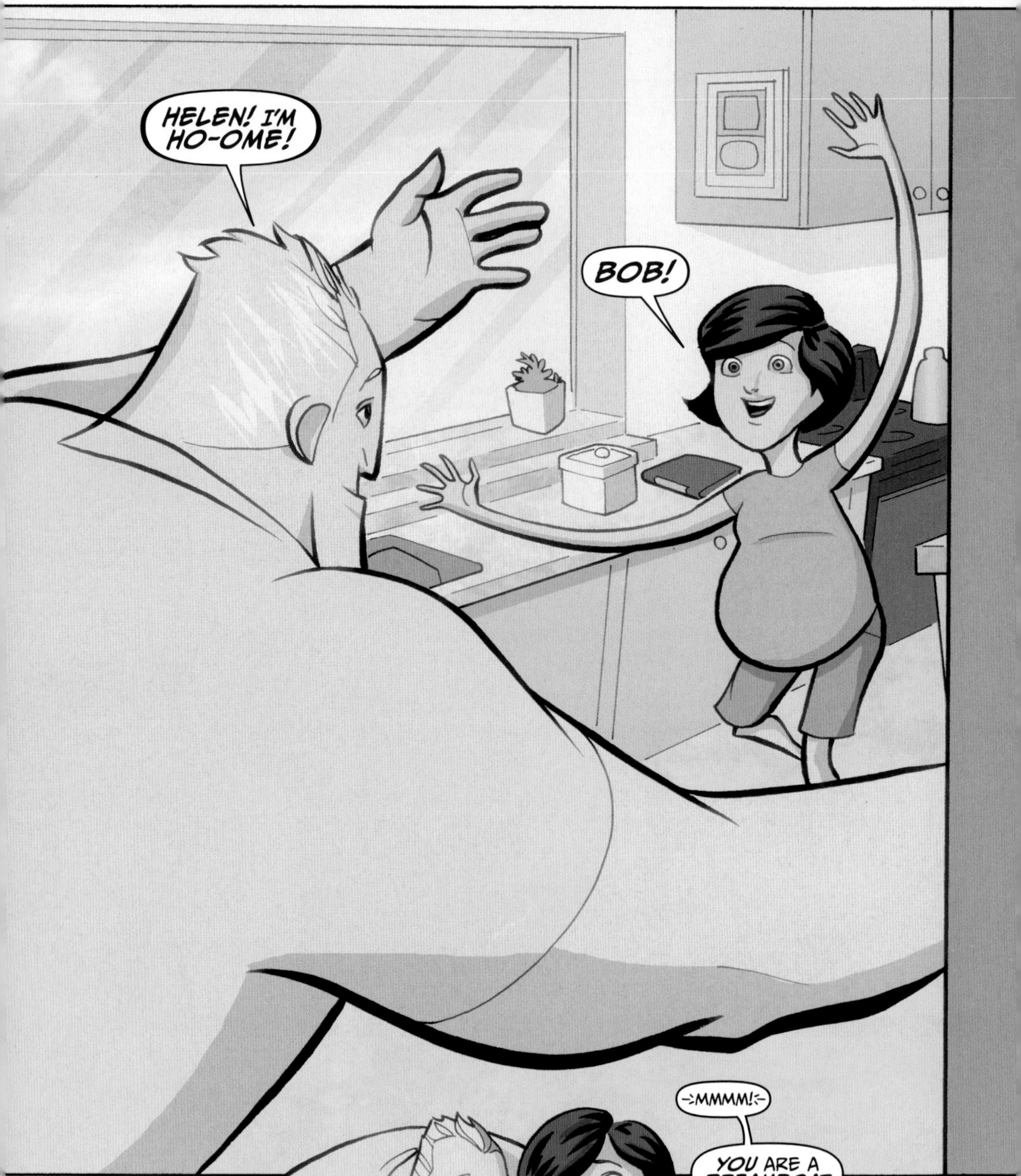
HELEN! I'M HO-OME!
BOB!

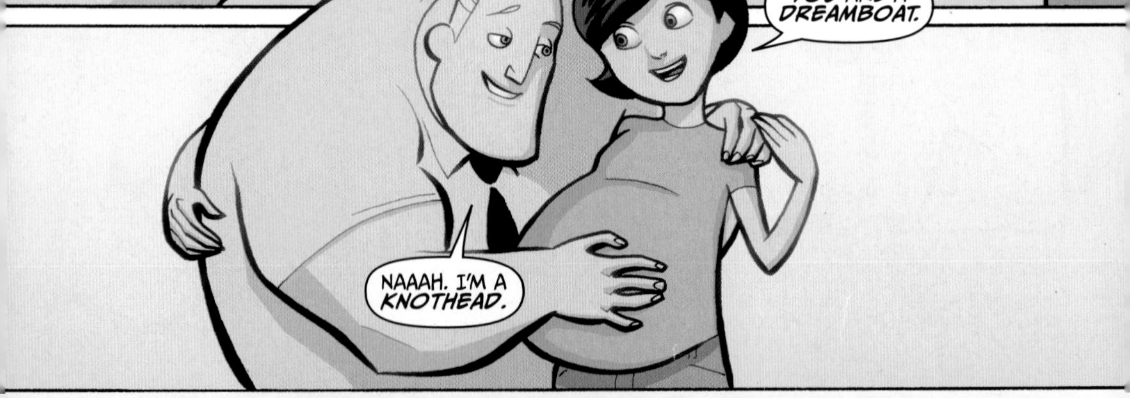
-MMMM!-
YOU ARE A DREAMBOAT.
NAAAH. I'M A KNOTHEAD.

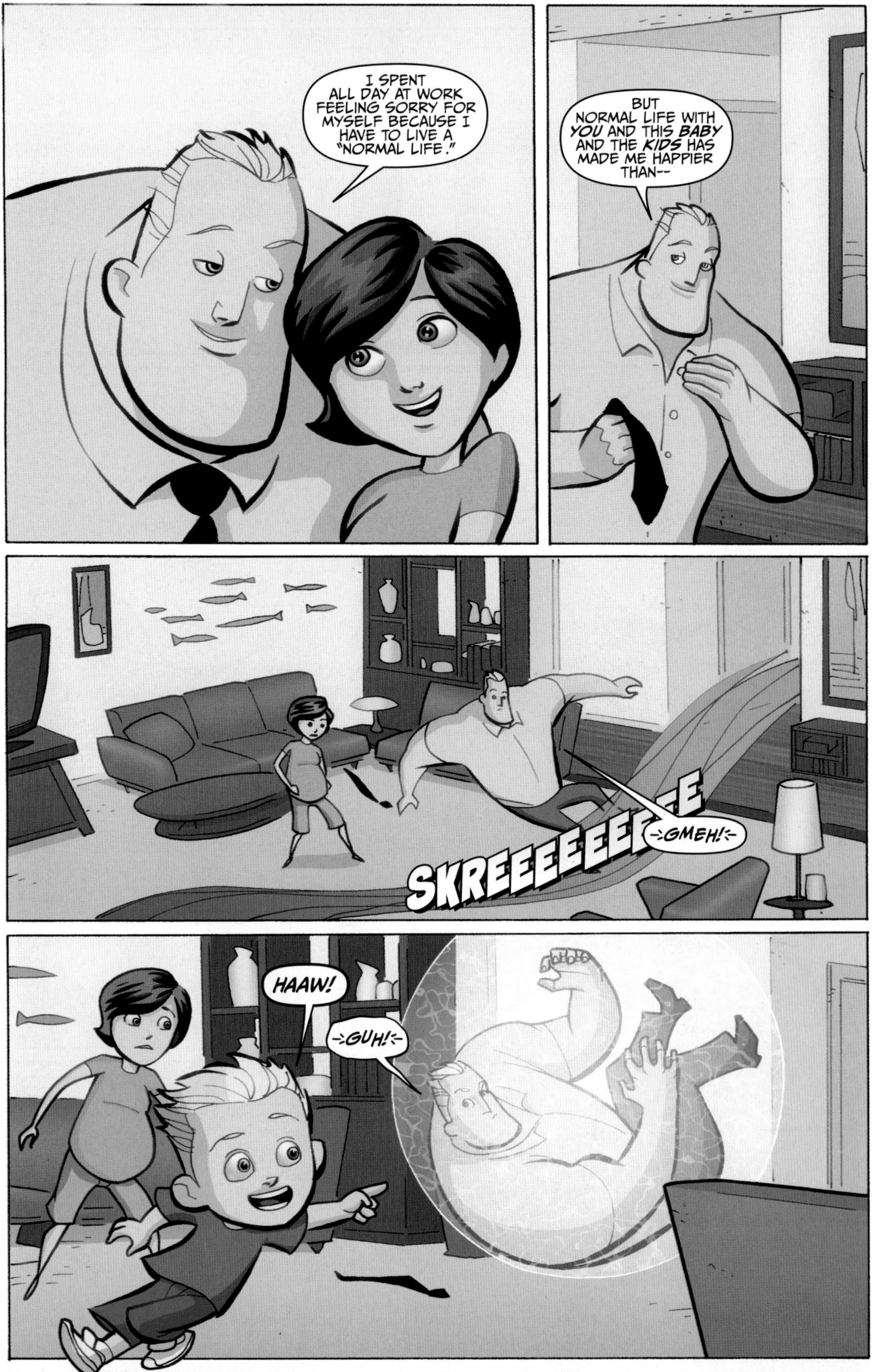
I SPENT ALL DAY AT WORK FEELING SORRY FOR MYSELF BECAUSE I HAVE TO LIVE A "NORMAL LIFE."
BUT NORMAL LIFE WITH *YOU* AND THIS *BABY* AND THE *KIDS* HAS MADE ME HAPPIER THAN--
-GMEH!-
SKREEEEEEEEEE
HAAW!
-GUH!-

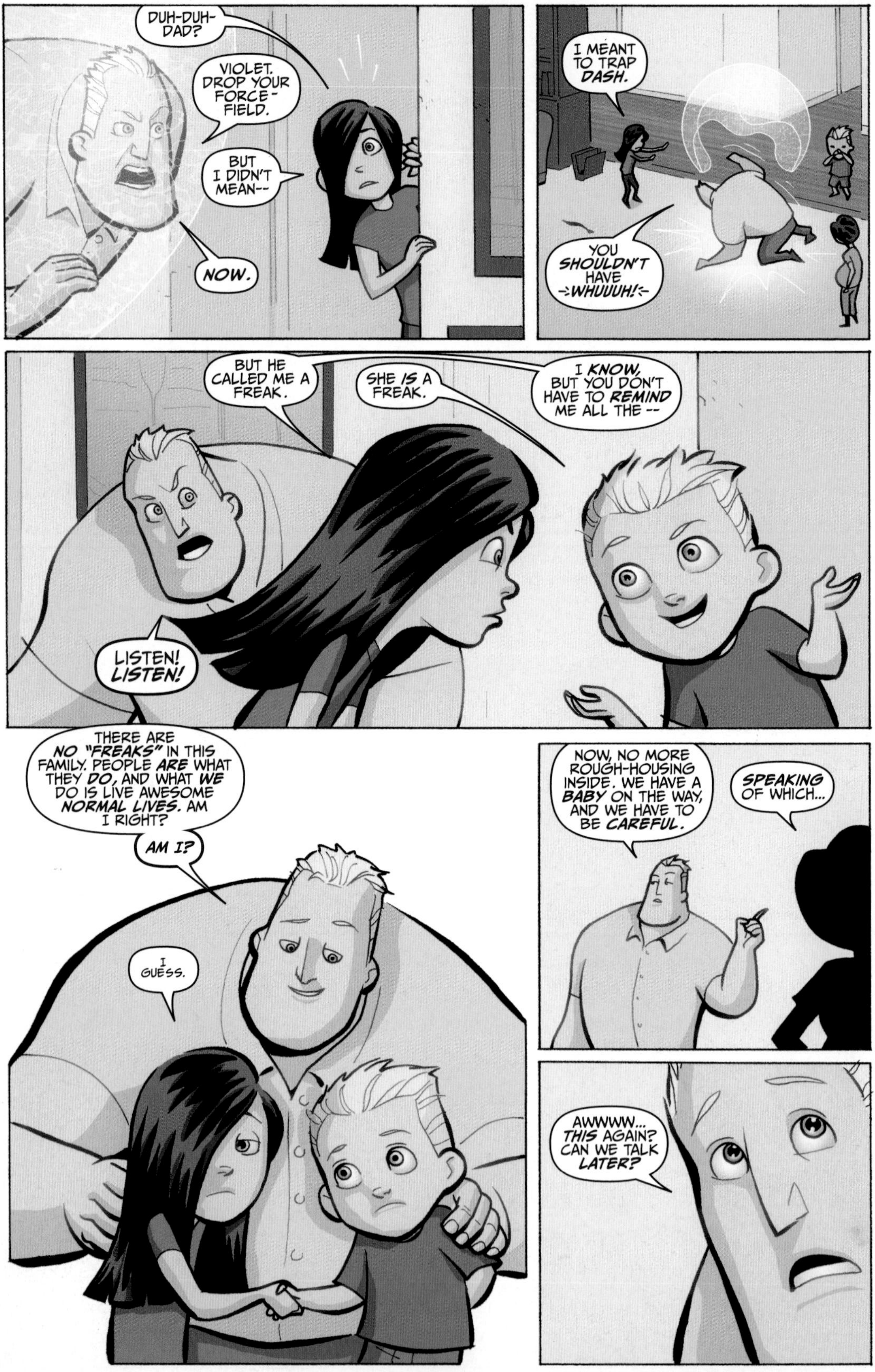
DUH-DUH-DUH-DAD?
VIOLET. DROP YOUR FORCE-FIELD.
BUT I DIDN'T MEAN--
NOW.
I MEANT TO TRAP DASH.
YOU SHOULDN'T HAVE -WHUUUH!-
BUT HE CALLED ME A FREAK.
SHE IS A FREAK.
I KNOW, BUT YOU DON'T HAVE TO REMIND ME ALL THE --
LISTEN! LISTEN!
THERE ARE NO "FREAKS" IN THIS FAMILY. PEOPLE ARE WHAT THEY DO, AND WHAT WE DO IS LIVE AWESOME NORMAL LIVES. AM I RIGHT?
AM I?
I GUESS.
NOW, NO MORE ROUGH-HOUSING INSIDE. WE HAVE A BABY ON THE WAY, AND WE HAVE TO BE CAREFUL.
SPEAKING OF WHICH...
AWWWW... THIS AGAIN? CAN WE TALK LATER?

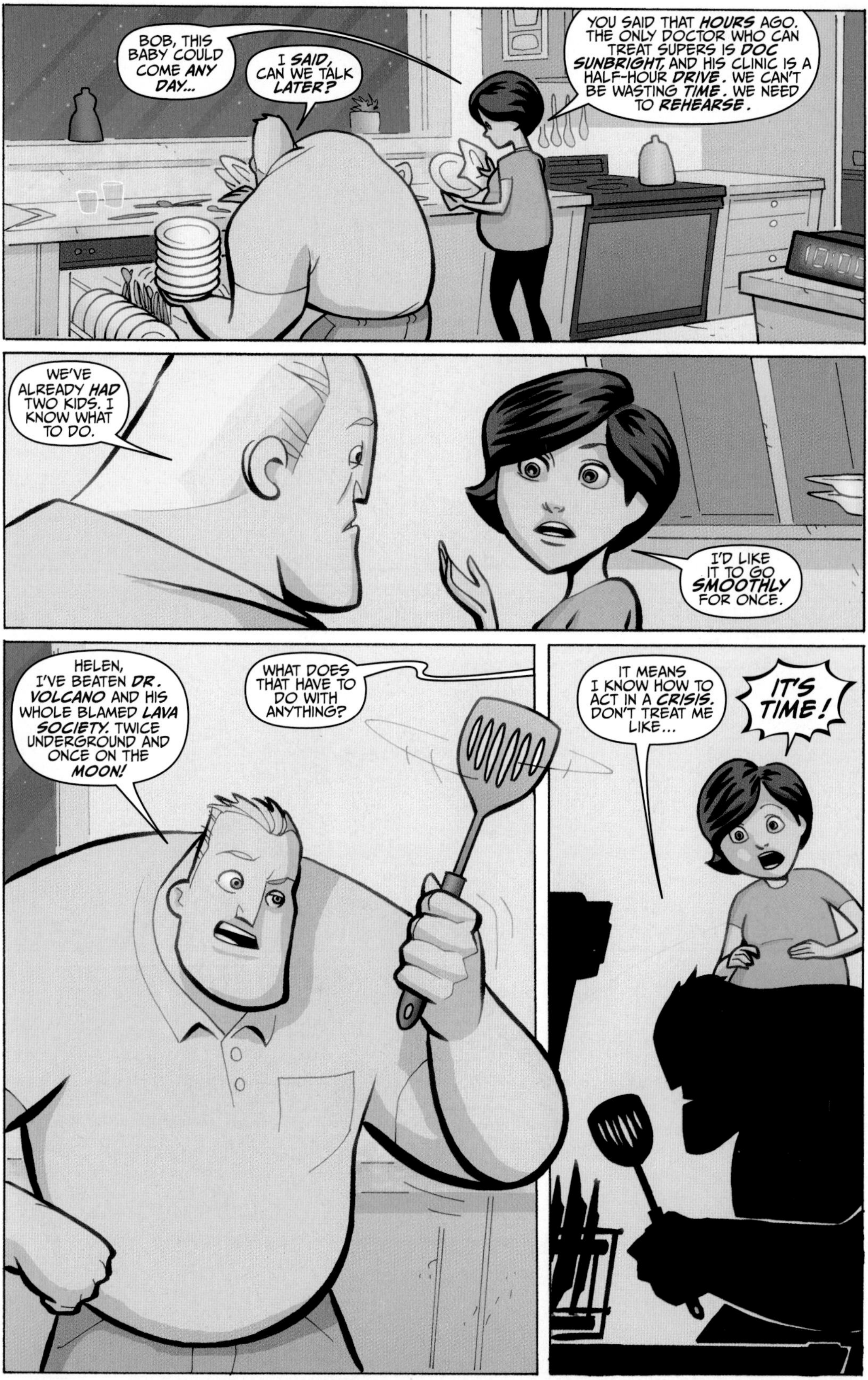
BOB, THIS BABY COULD COME **ANY DAY**...
I **SAID**, CAN WE TALK **LATER?**
YOU SAID THAT **HOURS** AGO. THE ONLY DOCTOR WHO CAN TREAT SUPERS IS **DOC SUNBRIGHT**, AND HIS CLINIC IS A HALF-HOUR **DRIVE**. WE CAN'T BE WASTING **TIME**. WE NEED TO **REHEARSE**.
WE'VE ALREADY **HAD** TWO KIDS. I KNOW WHAT TO DO.
I'D LIKE IT TO GO **SMOOTHLY** FOR ONCE.
HELEN, I'VE BEATEN **DR. VOLCANO** AND HIS WHOLE BLAMED **LAVA SOCIETY**. TWICE UNDERGROUND AND ONCE ON THE **MOON!**
WHAT DOES THAT HAVE TO DO WITH ANYTHING?
IT MEANS I KNOW HOW TO ACT IN A **CRISIS**. DON'T TREAT ME LIKE...
IT'S TIME!

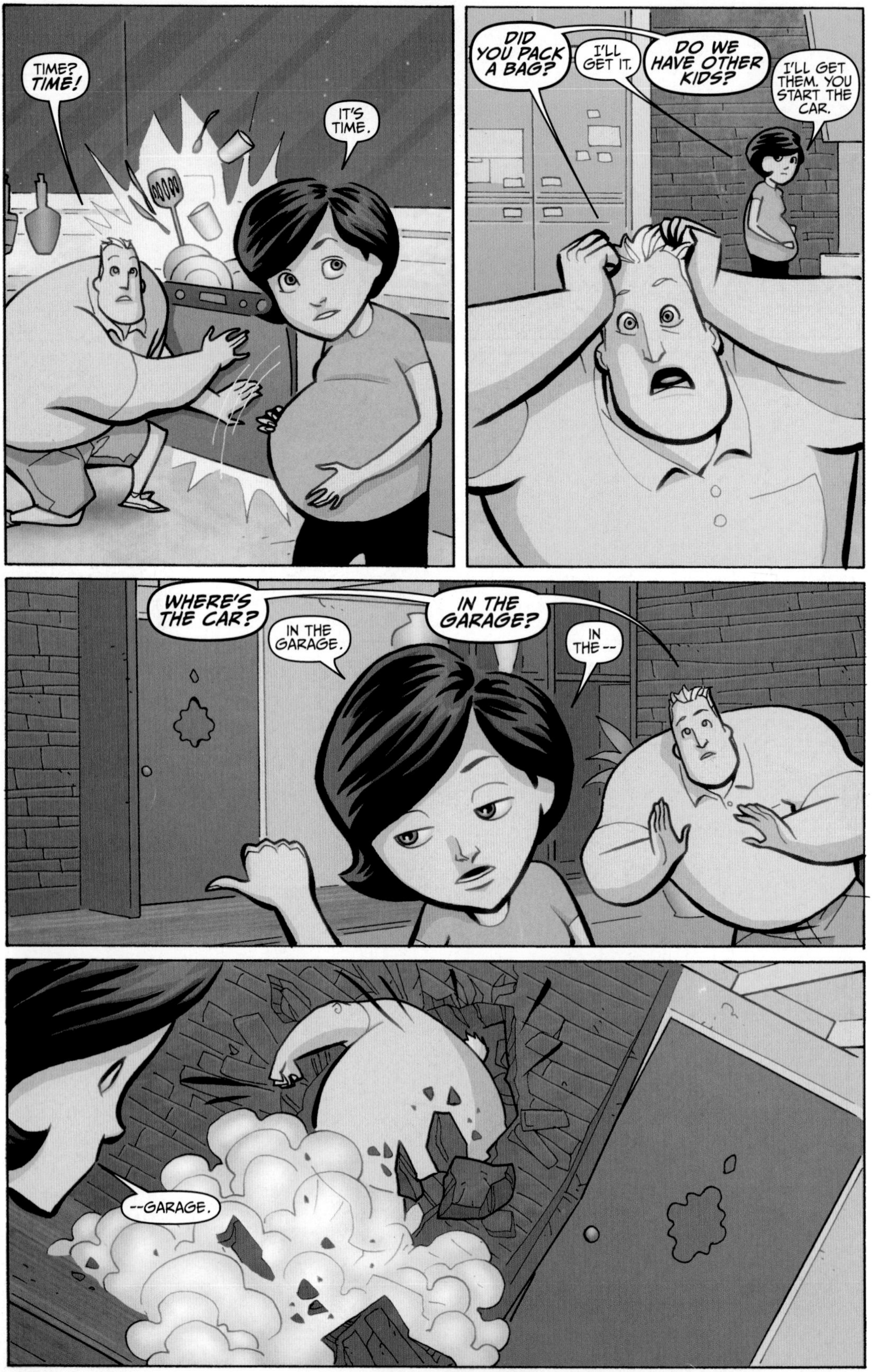
TIME? TIME!
IT'S TIME.
DID YOU PACK A BAG?
I'LL GET IT.
DO WE HAVE OTHER KIDS?
I'LL GET THEM. YOU START THE CAR.
WHERE'S THE CAR?
IN THE GARAGE.
IN THE GARAGE?
IN THE--
--GARAGE.

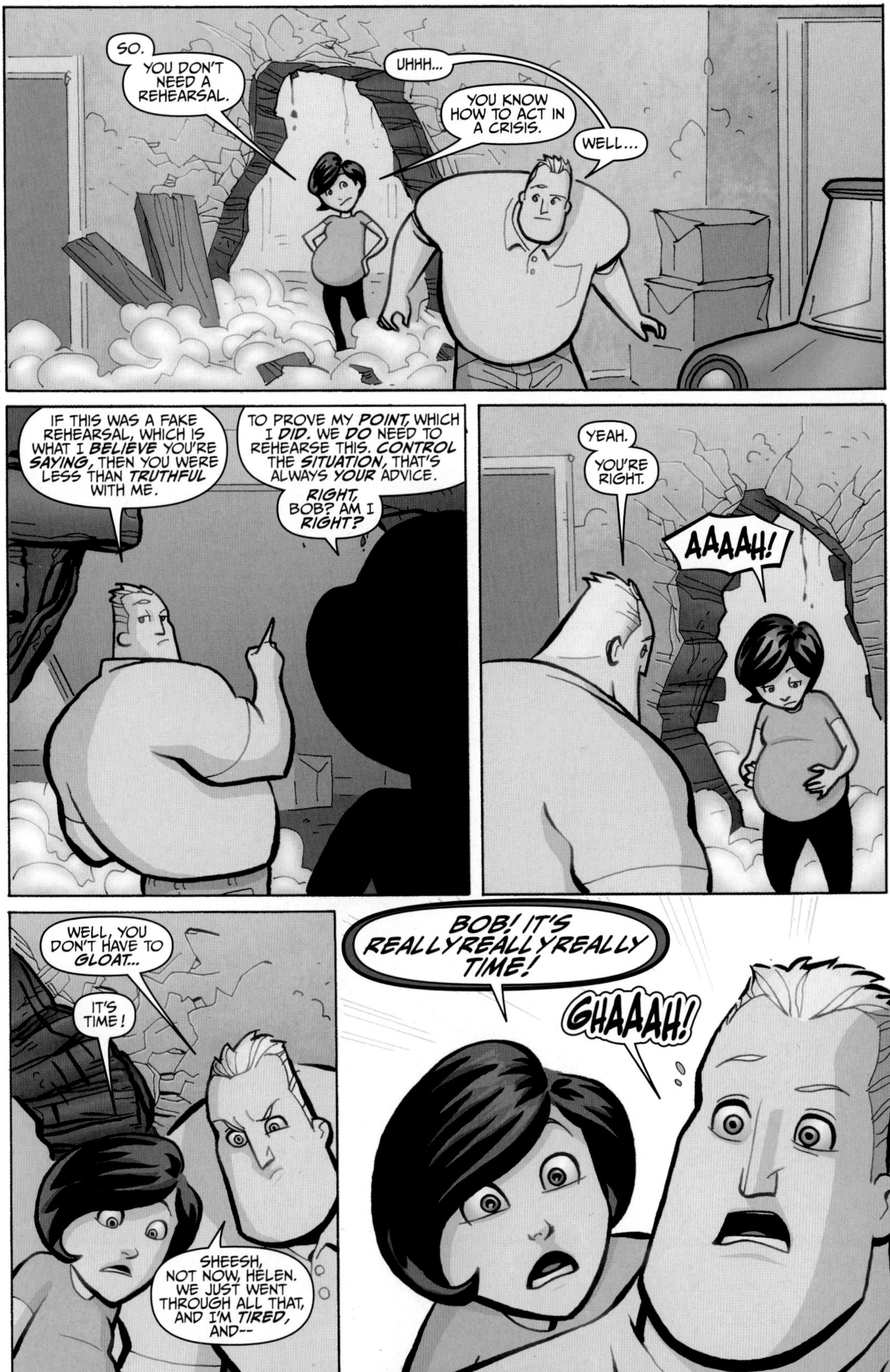
SO.
YOU DON'T NEED A REHEARSAL.
UHHH...
YOU KNOW HOW TO ACT IN A CRISIS.
WELL...
IF THIS WAS A FAKE REHEARSAL, WHICH IS WHAT I *BELIEVE* YOU'RE *SAYING*, THEN YOU WERE LESS THAN *TRUTHFUL* WITH ME.
TO PROVE MY *POINT*, WHICH I *DID*. WE *DO* NEED TO REHEARSE THIS. *CONTROL* THE *SITUATION*, THAT'S ALWAYS *YOUR* ADVICE.
RIGHT, BOB? AM I *RIGHT?*
YEAH.
YOU'RE RIGHT.
AAAAH!
WELL, YOU DON'T HAVE TO *GLOAT*...
IT'S TIME!
SHEESH, NOT NOW, HELEN. WE JUST WENT THROUGH ALL THAT, AND I'M *TIRED*, AND--
BOB! IT'S REALLYREALLYREALLY TIME!
GHAAAH!

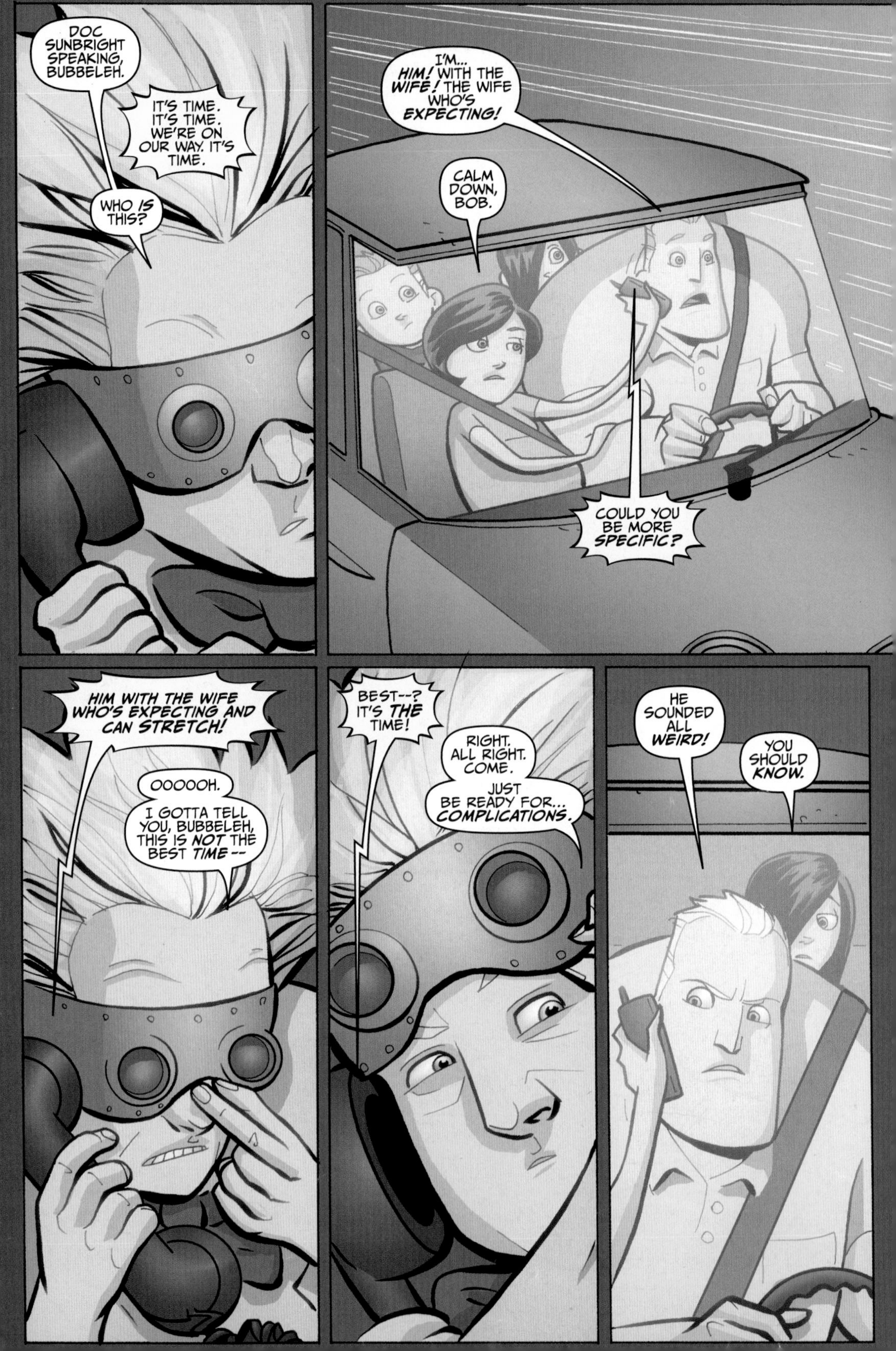
DOC SUNBRIGHT SPEAKING, BUBBELEH.
IT'S TIME. IT'S TIME. WE'RE ON OUR WAY. IT'S TIME.
WHO *IS* THIS?
I'M... *HIM!* WITH THE *WIFE!* THE WIFE WHO'S *EXPECTING!*
CALM DOWN, BOB.
COULD YOU BE MORE *SPECIFIC?*
HIM WITH THE WIFE WHO'S EXPECTING AND CAN STRETCH!
OOOOOH.
I GOTTA TELL YOU, BUBBELEH, THIS IS *NOT* THE BEST *TIME* --
BEST--? IT'S *THE* TIME!
RIGHT. ALL RIGHT. COME.
JUST BE READY FOR... *COMPLICATIONS*.
HE SOUNDED ALL *WEIRD!*
YOU SHOULD *KNOW*.

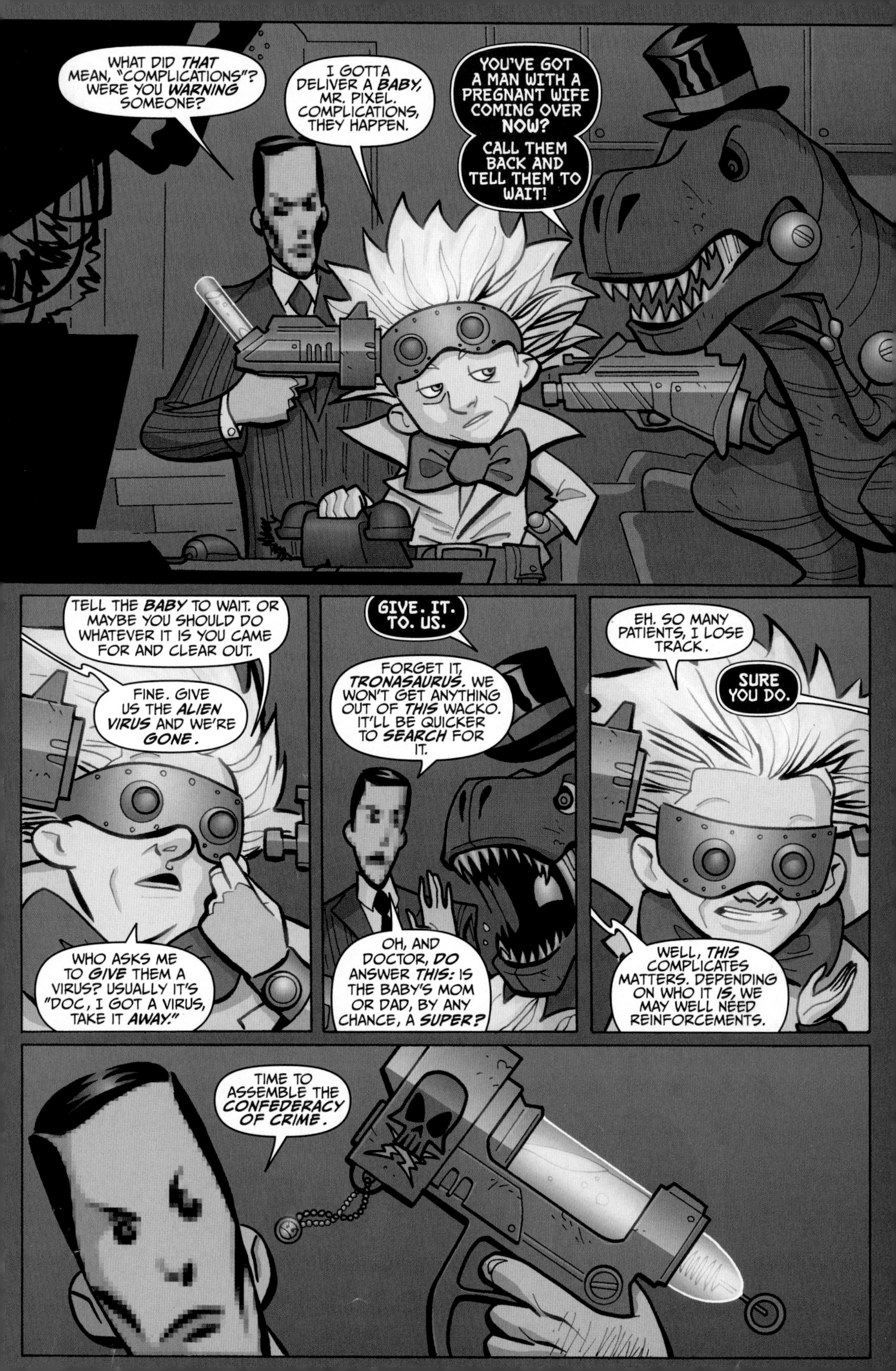
WHAT DID THAT MEAN, "COMPLICATIONS"? WERE YOU WARNING SOMEONE?
I GOTTA DELIVER A BABY, MR. PIXEL. COMPLICATIONS, THEY HAPPEN.
YOU'VE GOT A MAN WITH A PREGNANT WIFE COMING OVER NOW?
CALL THEM BACK AND TELL THEM TO WAIT!
TELL THE BABY TO WAIT. OR MAYBE YOU SHOULD DO WHATEVER IT IS YOU CAME FOR AND CLEAR OUT.
FINE. GIVE US THE ALIEN VIRUS AND WE'RE GONE.
WHO ASKS ME TO GIVE THEM A VIRUS? USUALLY IT'S "DOC, I GOT A VIRUS, TAKE IT AWAY."
GIVE. IT. TO. US.
FORGET IT, TRONASAURUS. WE WON'T GET ANYTHING OUT OF THIS WACKO. IT'LL BE QUICKER TO SEARCH FOR IT.
OH, AND DOCTOR, DO ANSWER THIS: IS THE BABY'S MOM OR DAD, BY ANY CHANCE, A SUPER?
EH. SO MANY PATIENTS, I LOSE TRACK.
SURE YOU DO.
WELL, THIS COMPLICATES MATTERS. DEPENDING ON WHO IT IS, WE MAY WELL NEED REINFORCEMENTS.
TIME TO ASSEMBLE THE CONFEDERACY OF CRIME.

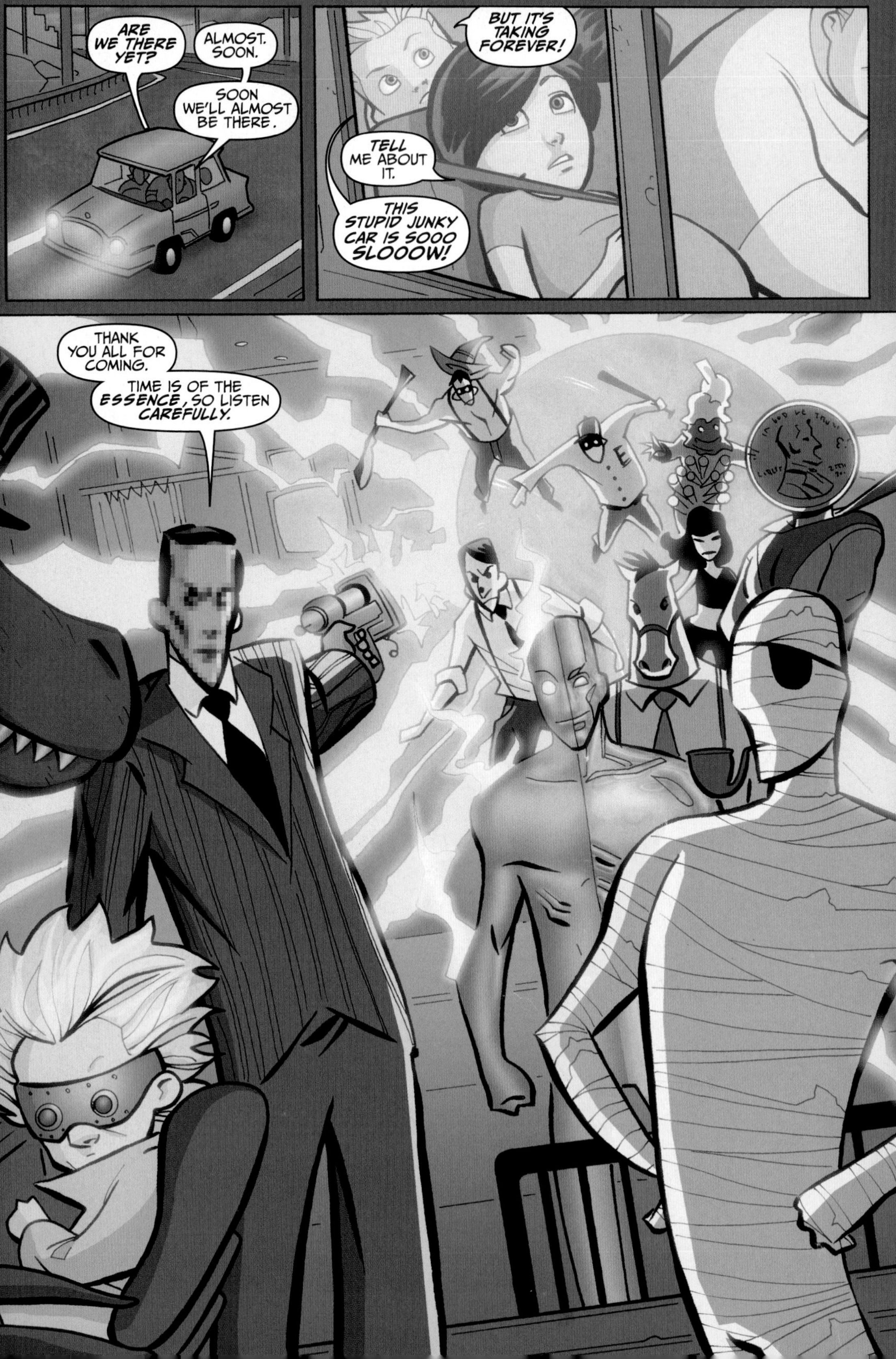
ARE WE THERE YET?
ALMOST. SOON.
SOON WE'LL ALMOST BE THERE.
BUT IT'S TAKING FOREVER!
TELL ME ABOUT IT.
THIS STUPID JUNKY CAR IS SOOO SLOOOW!
THANK YOU ALL FOR COMING.
TIME IS OF THE ESSENCE, SO LISTEN CAREFULLY.

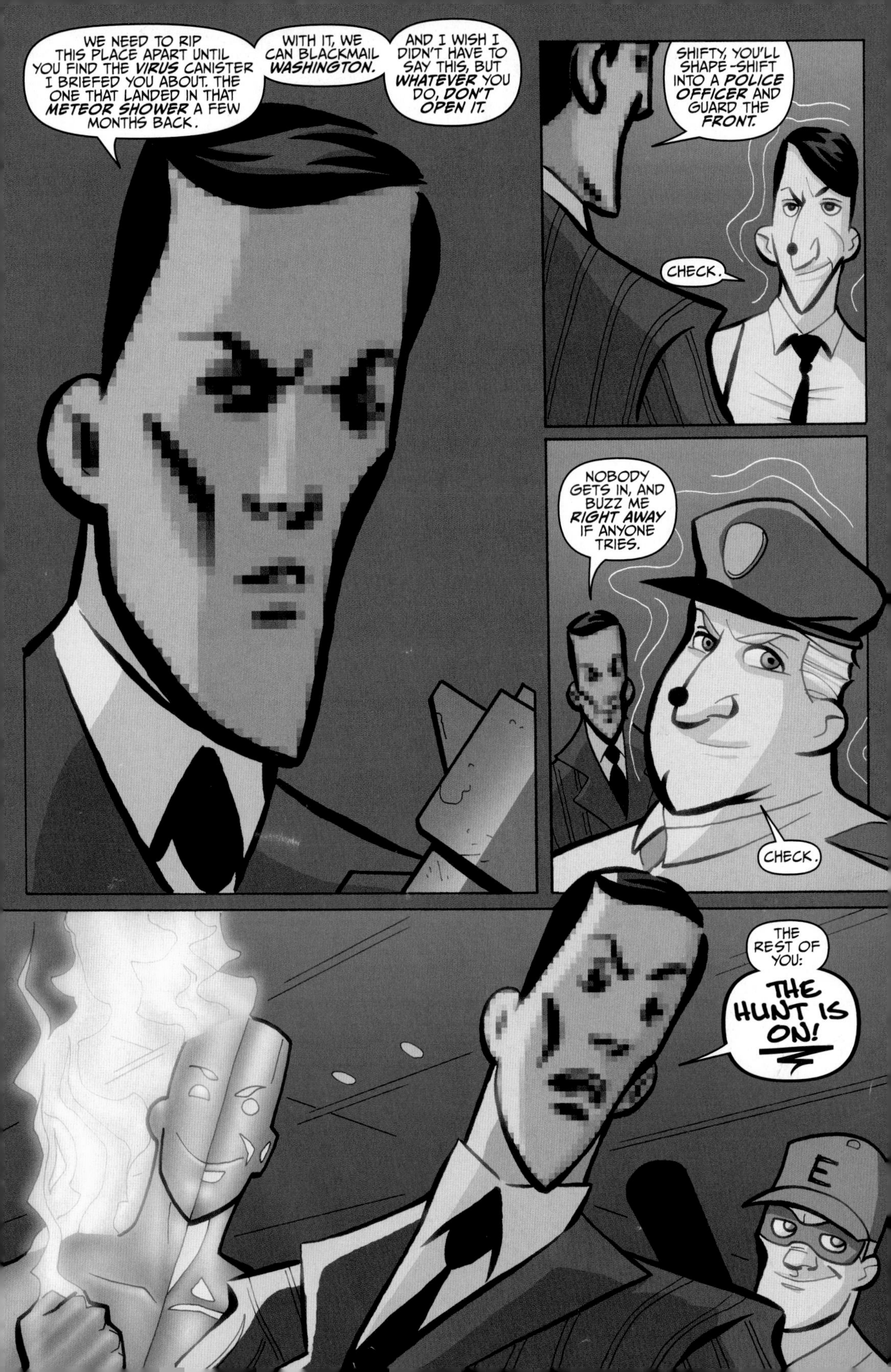
WE NEED TO RIP THIS PLACE APART UNTIL YOU FIND THE VIRUS CANISTER I BRIEFED YOU ABOUT. THE ONE THAT LANDED IN THAT METEOR SHOWER A FEW MONTHS BACK.
WITH IT, WE CAN BLACKMAIL WASHINGTON.
AND I WISH I DIDN'T HAVE TO SAY THIS, BUT WHATEVER YOU DO, DON'T OPEN IT.
SHIFTY, YOU'LL SHAPE-SHIFT INTO A POLICE OFFICER AND GUARD THE FRONT.
CHECK.
NOBODY GETS IN, AND BUZZ ME RIGHT AWAY IF ANYONE TRIES.
CHECK.
THE REST OF YOU:
THE HUNT IS ON!

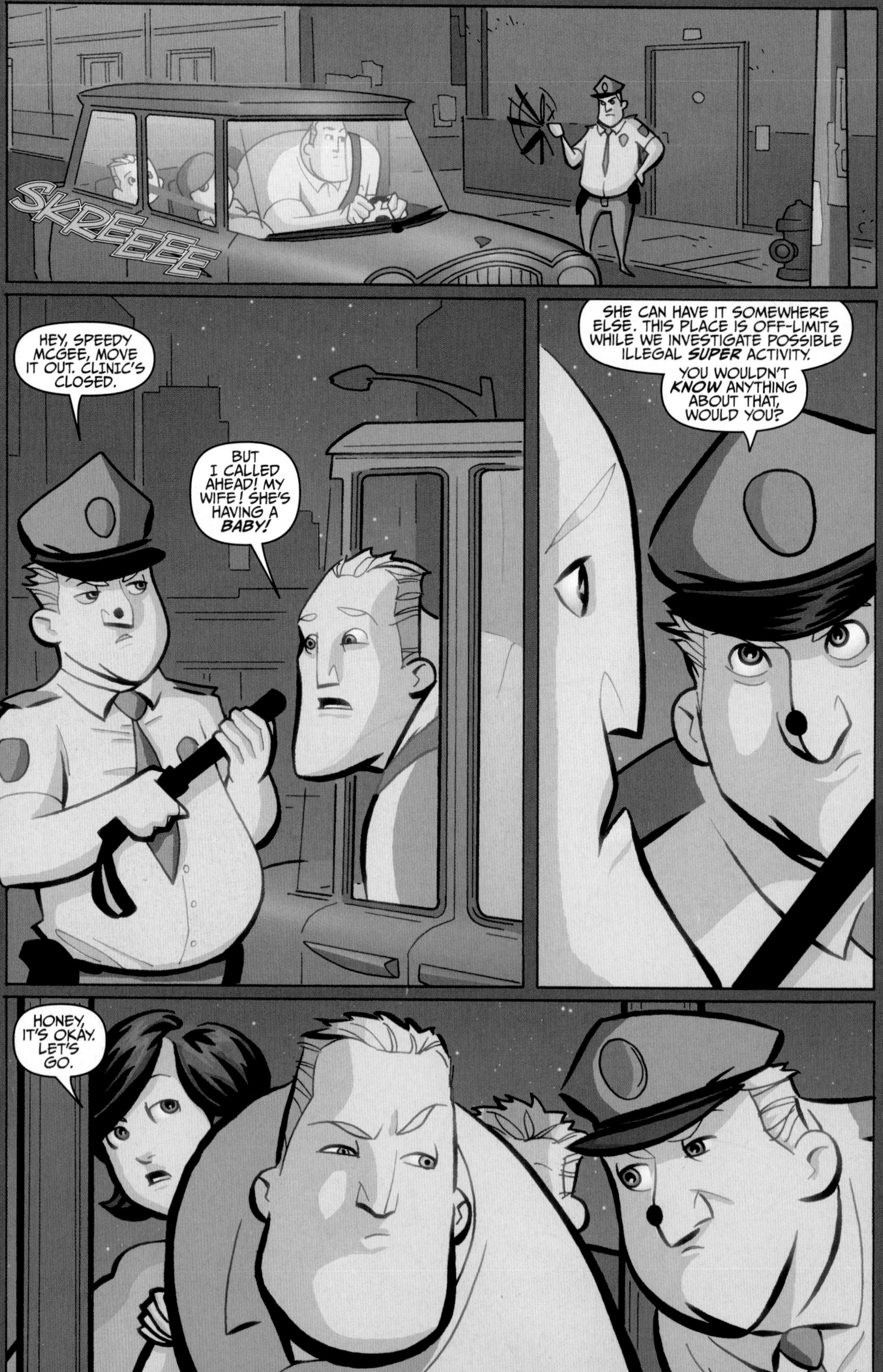
SKREEEEE
HEY, SPEEDY MCGEE, MOVE IT OUT. CLINIC'S CLOSED.
BUT I CALLED AHEAD! MY WIFE! SHE'S HAVING A BABY!
SHE CAN HAVE IT SOMEWHERE ELSE. THIS PLACE IS OFF-LIMITS WHILE WE INVESTIGATE POSSIBLE ILLEGAL SUPER ACTIVITY.
YOU WOULDN'T KNOW ANYTHING ABOUT THAT, WOULD YOU?
HONEY, IT'S OKAY. LET'S GO.

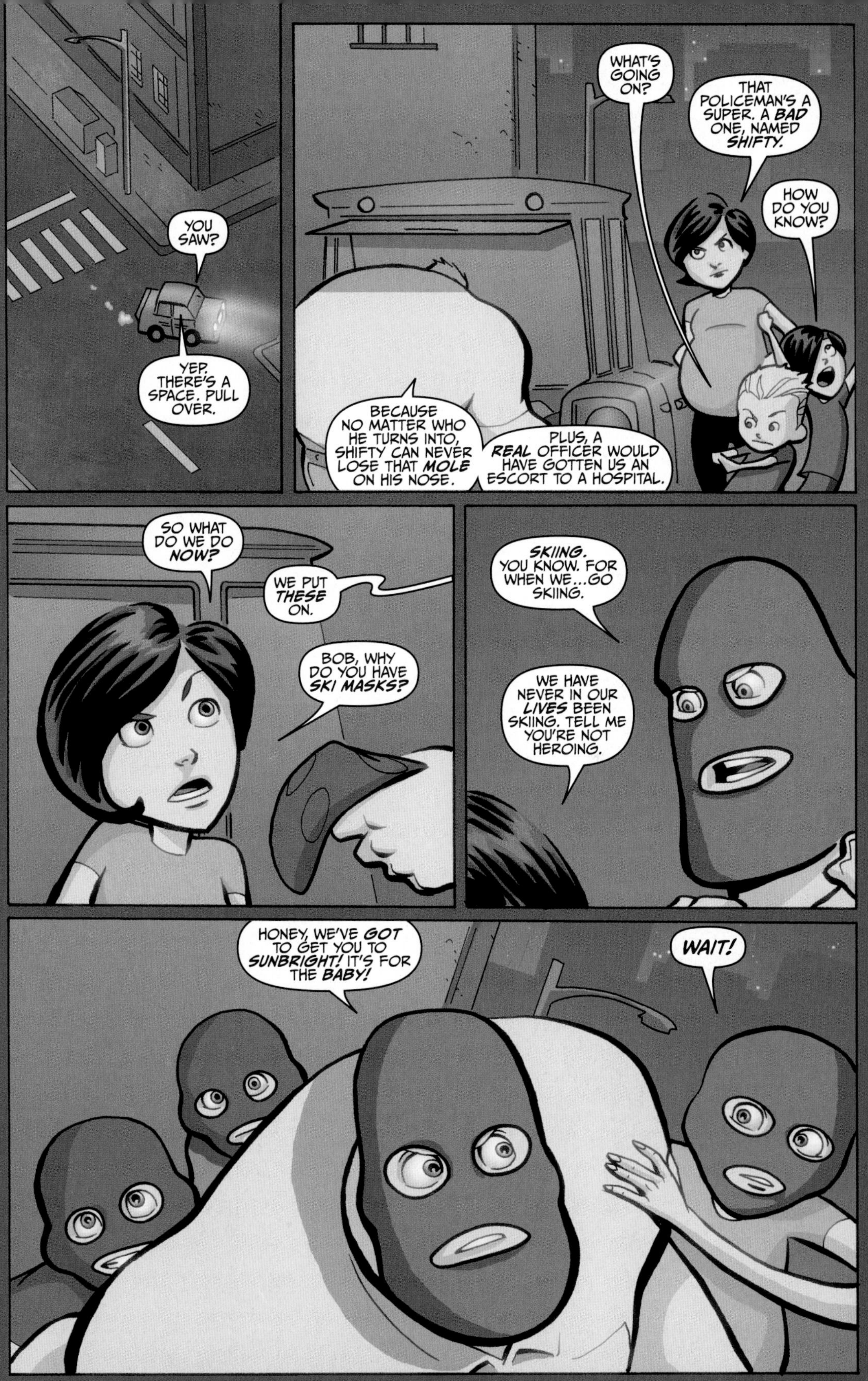

YOU SAW?
YEP. THERE'S A SPACE. PULL OVER.
WHAT'S GOING ON?
THAT POLICEMAN'S A SUPER. A BAD ONE, NAMED SHIFTY.
HOW DO YOU KNOW?
BECAUSE NO MATTER WHO HE TURNS INTO, SHIFTY CAN NEVER LOSE THAT MOLE ON HIS NOSE.
PLUS, A REAL OFFICER WOULD HAVE GOTTEN US AN ESCORT TO A HOSPITAL.
SO WHAT DO WE DO NOW?
WE PUT THESE ON.
BOB, WHY DO YOU HAVE SKI MASKS?
SKIING. YOU KNOW. FOR WHEN WE...GO SKIING.
WE HAVE NEVER IN OUR LIVES BEEN SKIING. TELL ME YOU'RE NOT HEROING.
HONEY, WE'VE GOT TO GET YOU TO SUNBRIGHT! IT'S FOR THE BABY!
WAIT!

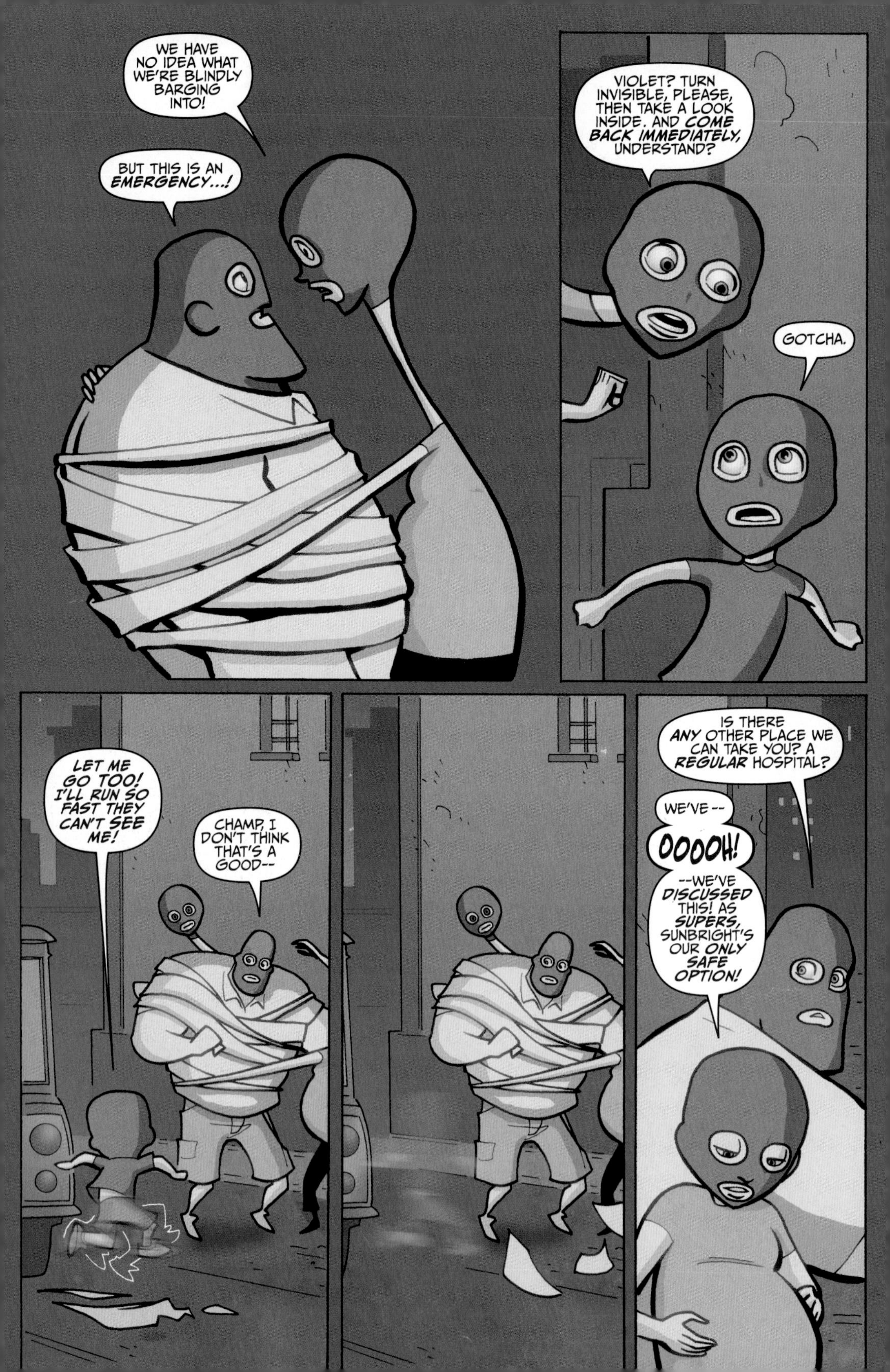
WE HAVE NO IDEA WHAT WE'RE BLINDLY BARGING INTO!
BUT THIS IS AN EMERGENCY...!
VIOLET? TURN INVISIBLE, PLEASE, THEN TAKE A LOOK INSIDE. AND COME BACK IMMEDIATELY, UNDERSTAND?
GOTCHA.
LET ME GO TOO! I'LL RUN SO FAST THEY CAN'T SEE ME!
CHAMP, I DON'T THINK THAT'S A GOOD--
IS THERE ANY OTHER PLACE WE CAN TAKE YOU? A REGULAR HOSPITAL?
WE'VE --
OOOOH!
--WE'VE DISCUSSED THIS! AS SUPERS, SUNBRIGHT'S OUR ONLY SAFE OPTION!

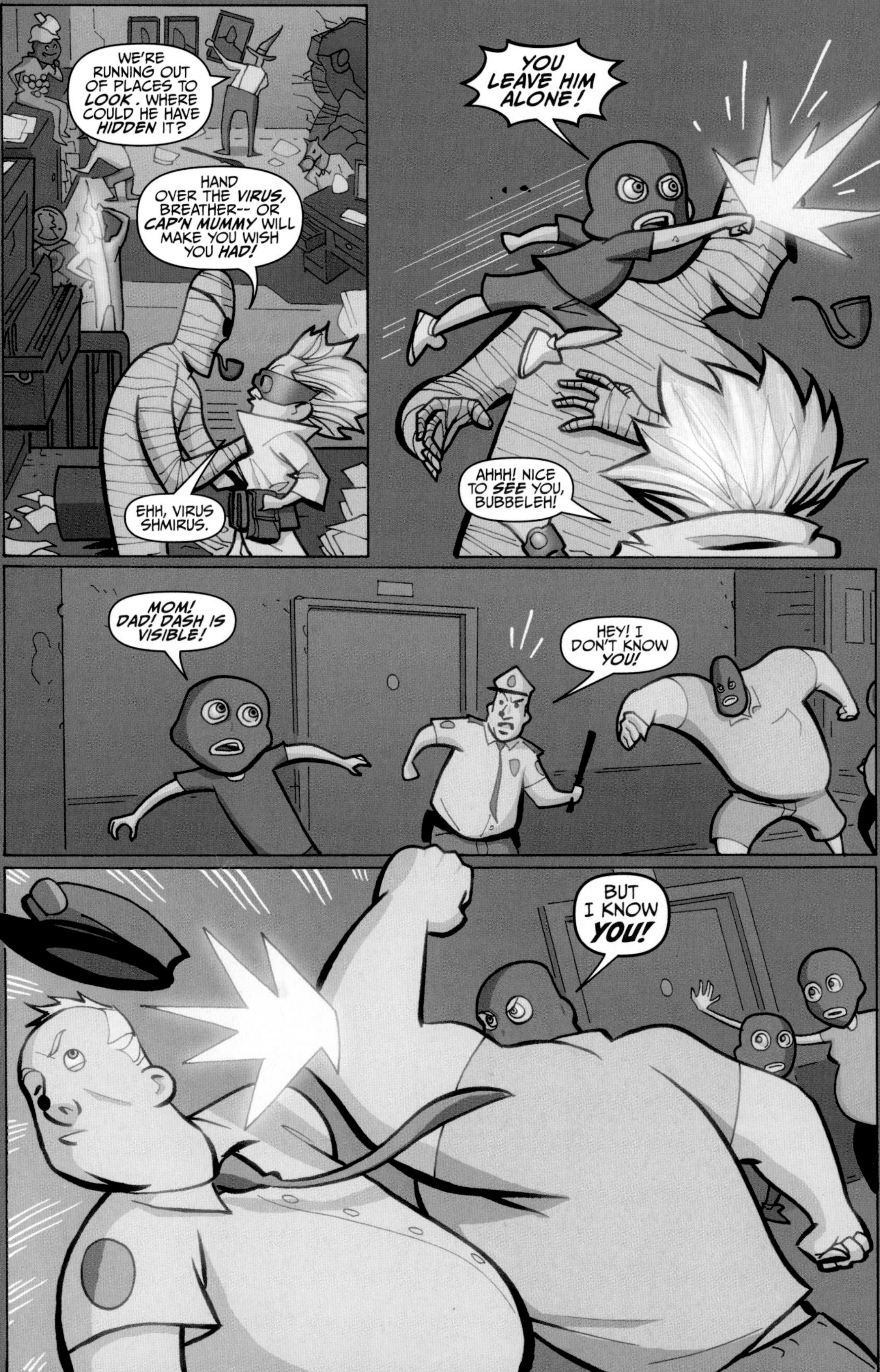

WE'RE RUNNING OUT OF PLACES TO LOOK. WHERE COULD HE HAVE HIDDEN IT?
HAND OVER THE VIRUS, BREATHER-- OR CAP'N MUMMY WILL MAKE YOU WISH YOU HAD!
EHH, VIRUS SHMIRUS.
YOU LEAVE HIM ALONE!
AHHH! NICE TO SEE YOU, BUBBELEH!
MOM! DAD! DASH IS VISIBLE!
HEY! I DON'T KNOW YOU!
BUT I KNOW YOU!

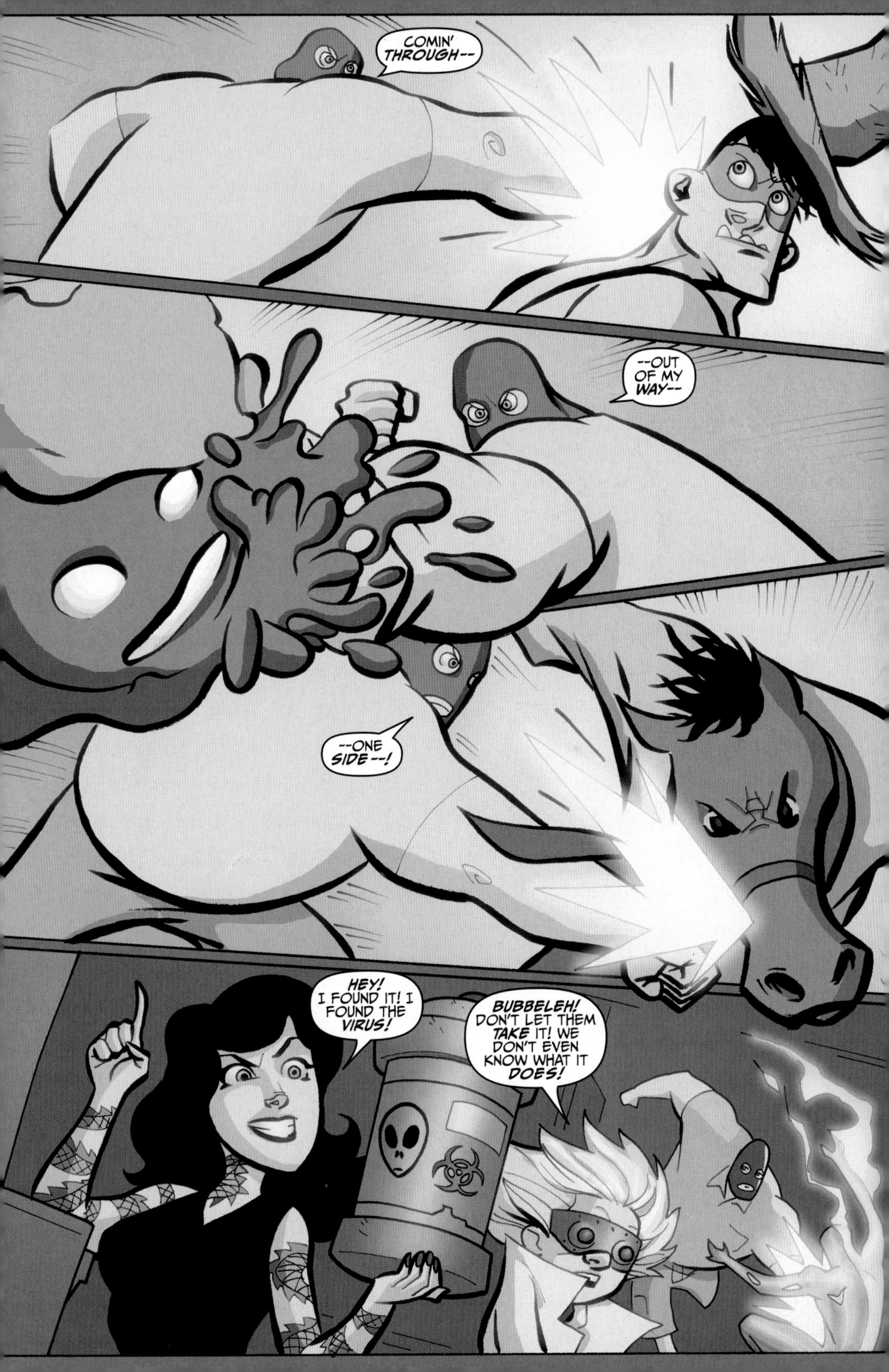
COMIN' THROUGH--
--OUT OF MY WAY--
--ONE SIDE--!
HEY! I FOUND IT! I FOUND THE VIRUS!
BUBBELEH! DON'T LET THEM TAKE IT! WE DON'T EVEN KNOW WHAT IT DOES!

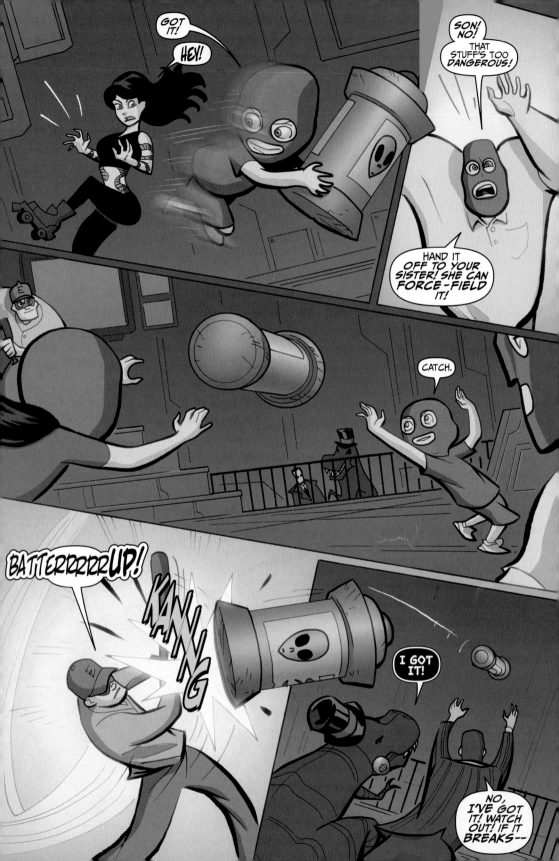

--WE'RE *ALL* LOSERS. NOT JUST *YOU* TWO.

DON'T TOUCH THAT!

NICE *SAVE*, BUBBIE, BUT THAT'S FULL OF *NASTY STUFF!* CANISTER OR *NO* CANISTER, IT SHOULD NOT BE *ANYWHERE* NEAR AN *EXPECTANT MOTHER!*

COME ON. LET THEM DO THEIR CRAZY FIGHTING.

WE'LL GO BRING A *LIFE* INTO THE WORLD.

SON! GET THE DOC AND YOUR MOM TO SAFETY *FAST!*

YES SIR!

NOW, WHERE'S MY DAUGHTER?

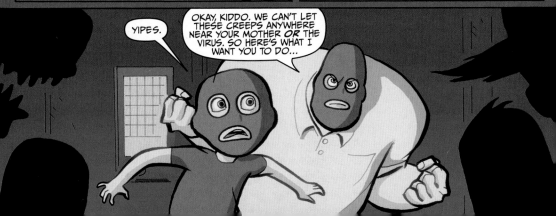

YIPES.

OKAY, KIDDO. WE CAN'T LET THESE CREEPS ANYWHERE NEAR YOUR MOTHER *OR* THE VIRUS. SO HERE'S WHAT I WANT YOU TO DO...

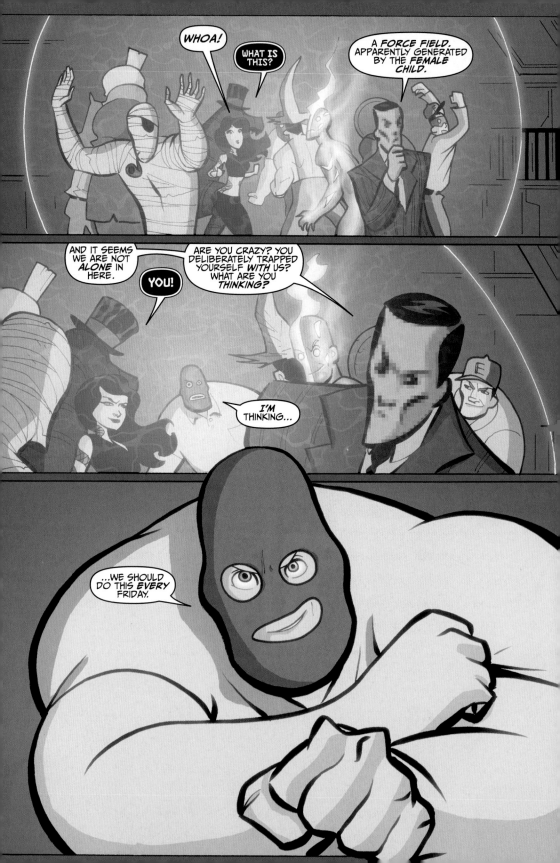

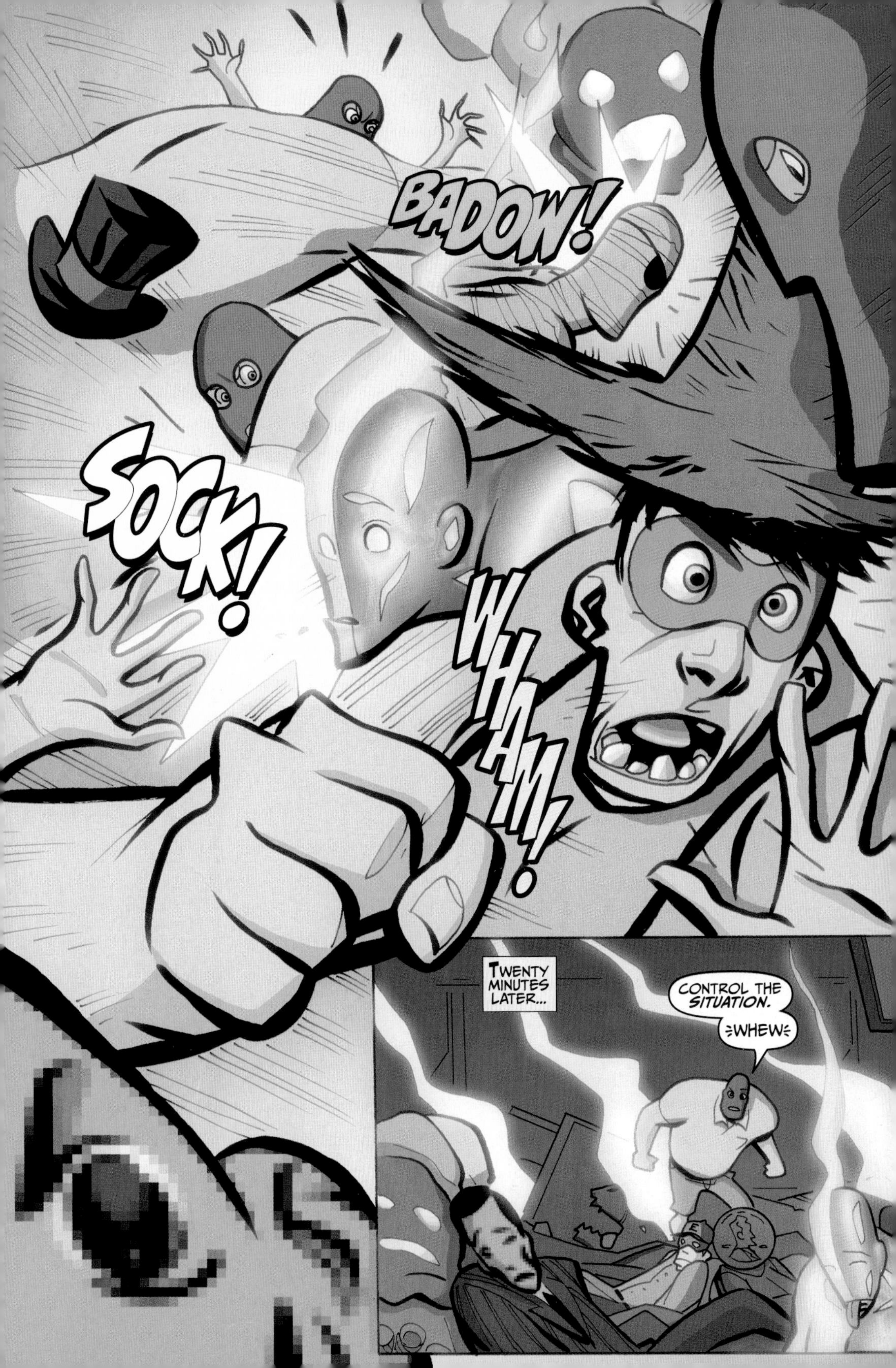
BADOW!
SOCK!
WHAM!
TWENTY MINUTES LATER...
CONTROL THE SITUATION.
WHEW

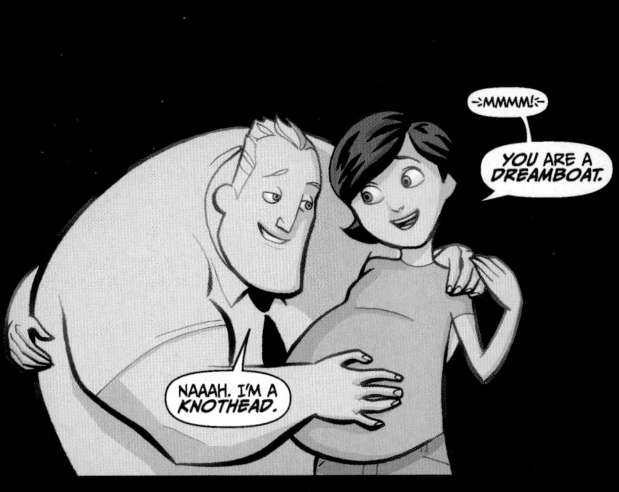
~MMMM!~
YOU ARE A DREAMBOAT.
NAAAH. I'M A KNOTHEAD.

CHAPTER ONE

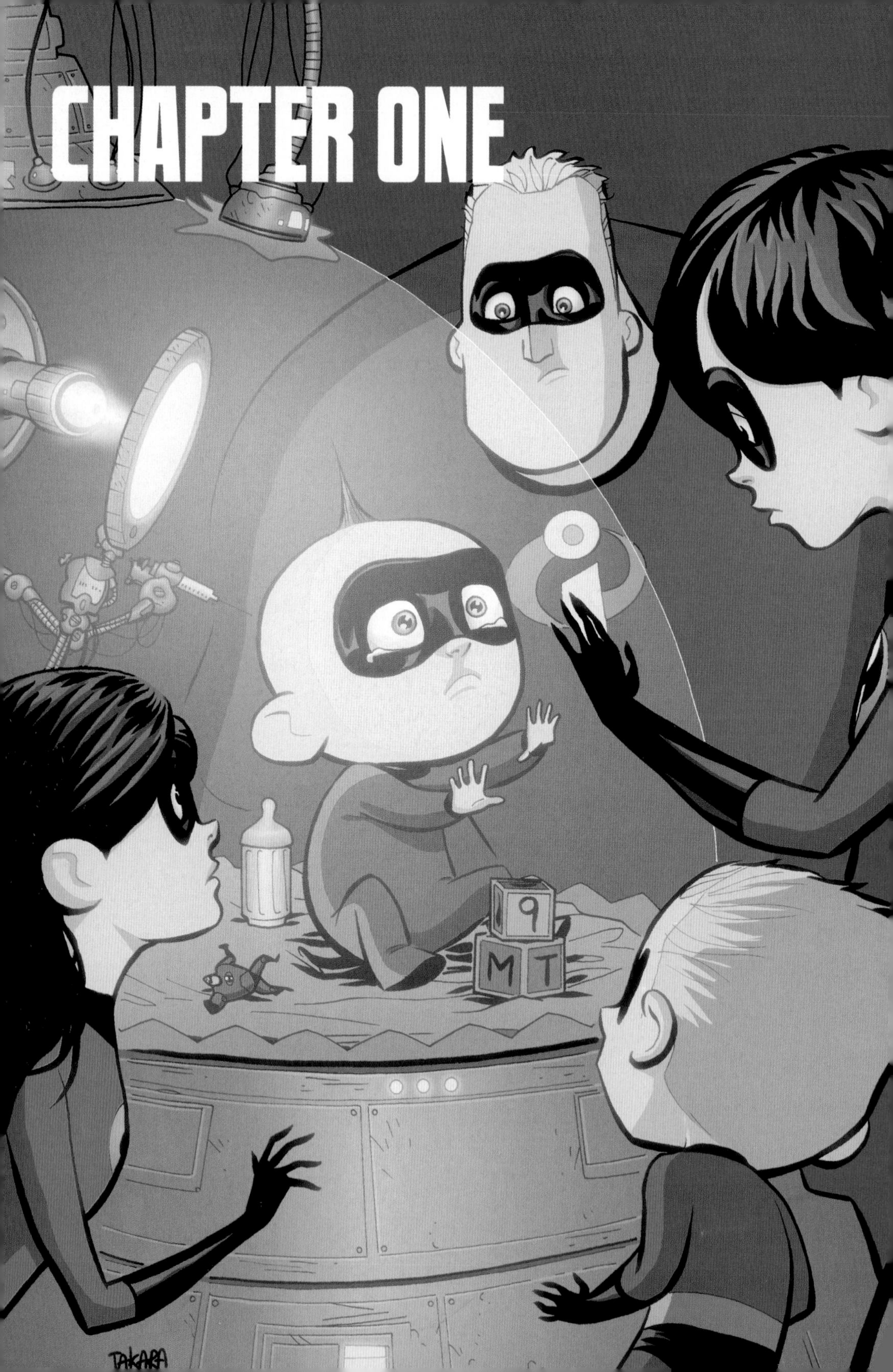
9
M T
TAKARA

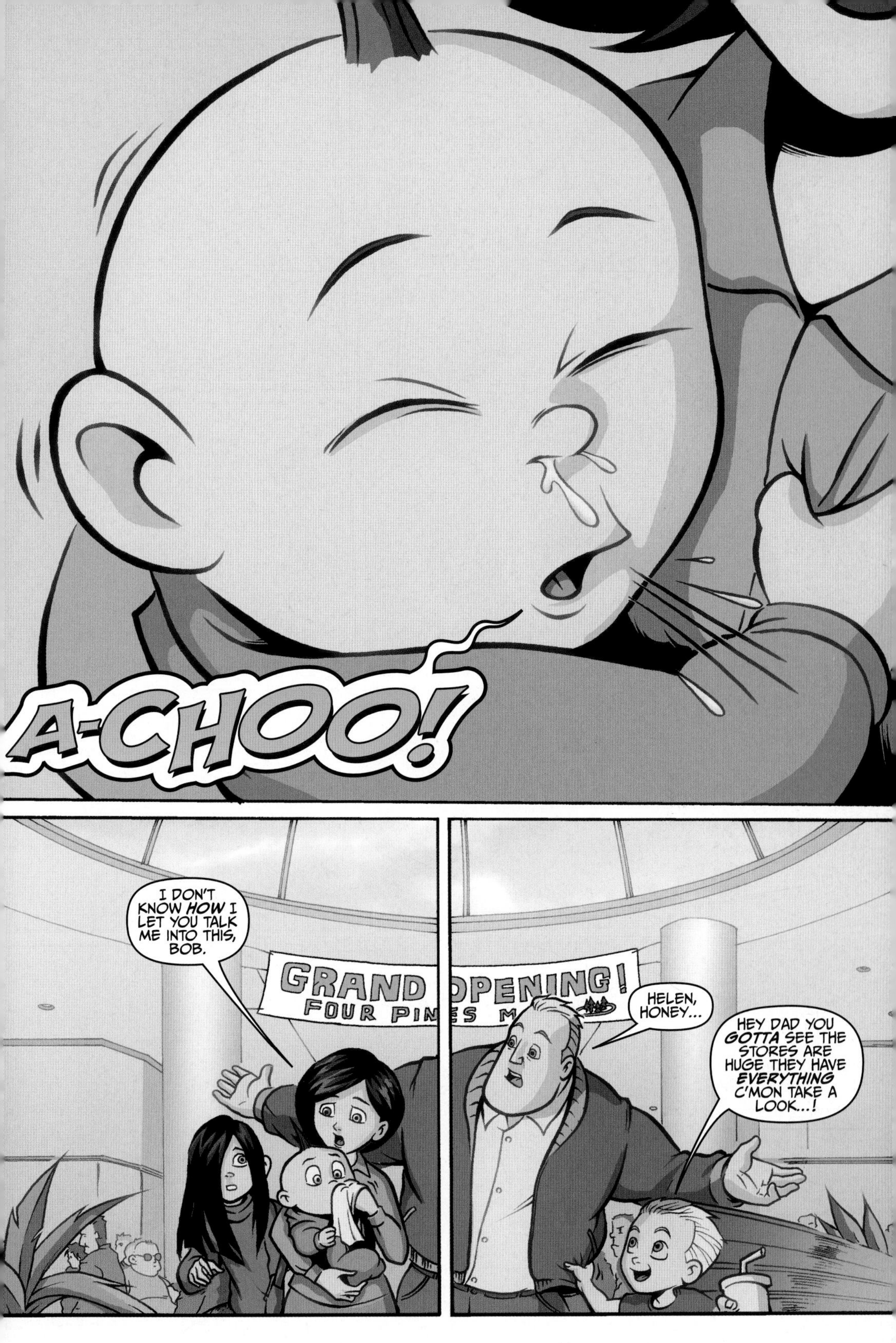
A-CHOO!
I DON'T KNOW *HOW* I LET YOU TALK ME INTO THIS, BOB.
GRAND OPENING!
FOUR PINES M
HELEN, HONEY...
HEY DAD YOU *GOTTA* SEE THE STORES ARE HUGE THEY HAVE *EVERYTHING* C'MON TAKE A LOOK...!

LATER.

GOTTA FIND JACK-JACK, GOTTA FIND JACK-JACK...

ERROR ERROR ERROR

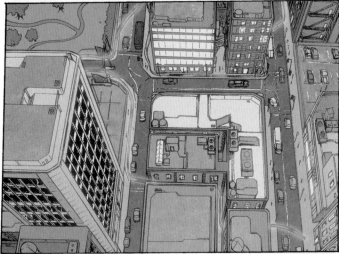

THE SECRET LABORATORY OF *DOCTOR SUNBRIGHT*.

...I DIDN'T FIND HIM... I CAN'T EVEN GET A *SIGNAL* WITH THIS PIECE OF JUNK...

IT'S *MY* FAULT...

THAT'S *STUPID!*

BUT...

WE WERE IN A MALL *FALLING* FROM THE SKY FILLED WITH *BAD GUYS!* IT'S NOT YOUR FAULT!

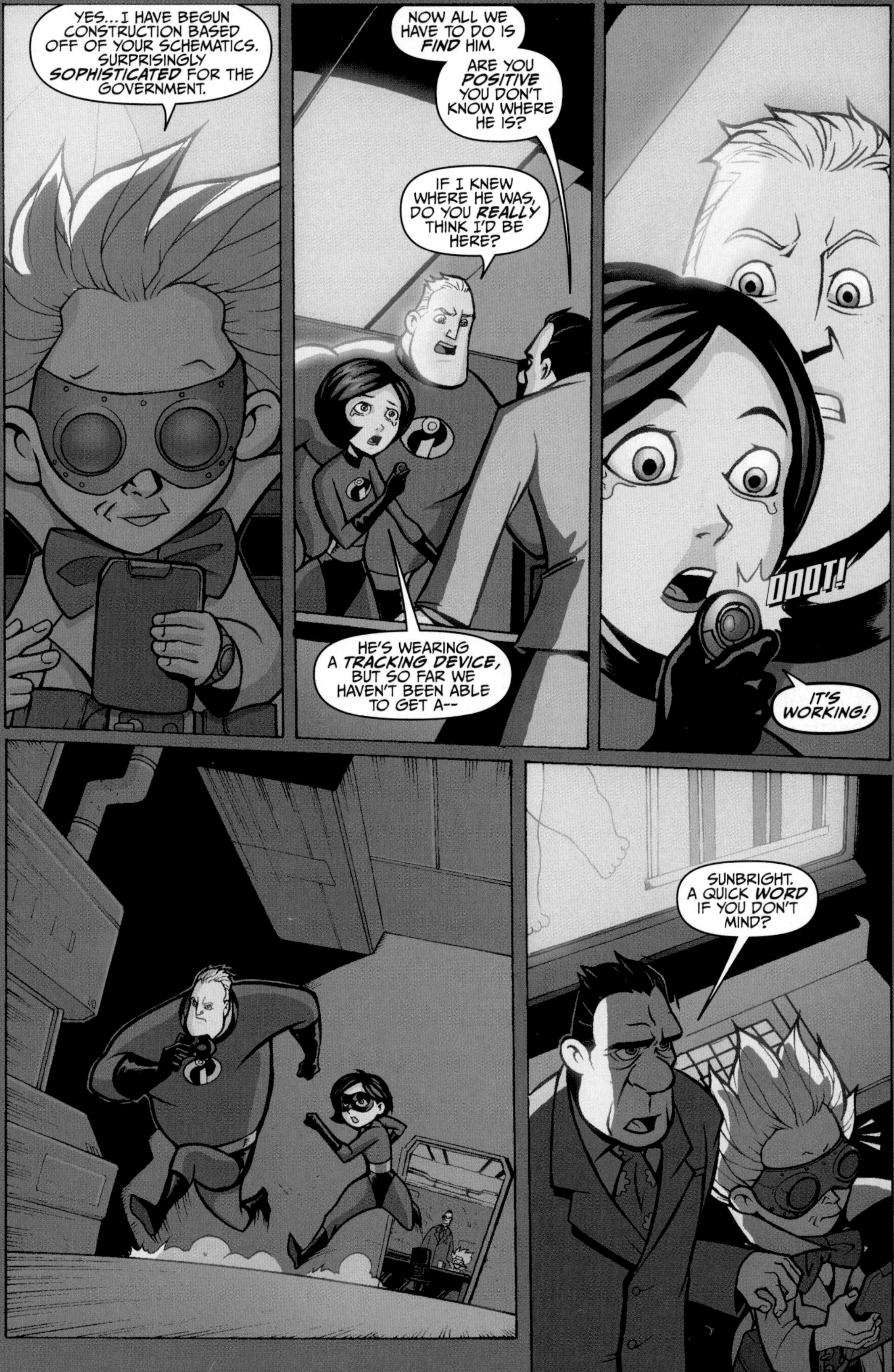
YES... I HAVE BEGUN CONSTRUCTION BASED OFF OF YOUR SCHEMATICS. SURPRISINGLY *SOPHISTICATED* FOR THE GOVERNMENT.
NOW ALL WE HAVE TO DO IS *FIND* HIM.
ARE YOU *POSITIVE* YOU DON'T KNOW WHERE HE IS?
IF I KNEW WHERE HE WAS, DO YOU *REALLY* THINK I'D BE HERE?
HE'S WEARING A *TRACKING DEVICE,* BUT SO FAR WE HAVEN'T BEEN ABLE TO GET A--
DOOT!
IT'S WORKING!
SUNBRIGHT. A QUICK *WORD* IF YOU DON'T MIND?

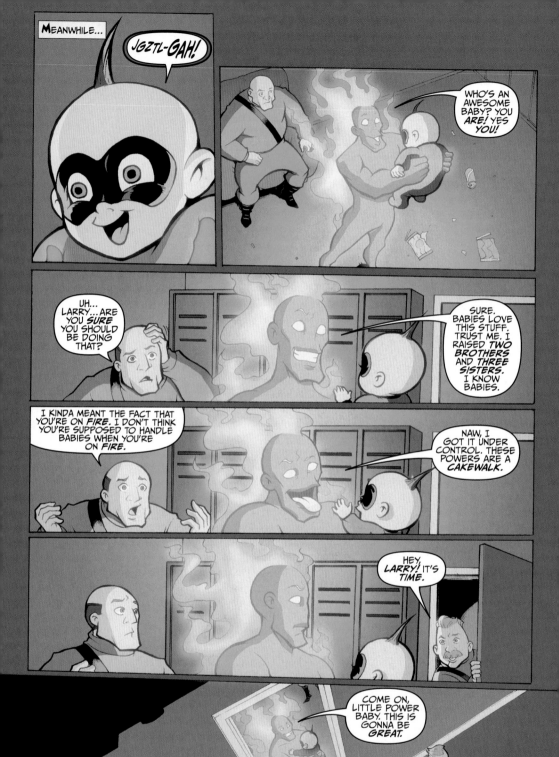

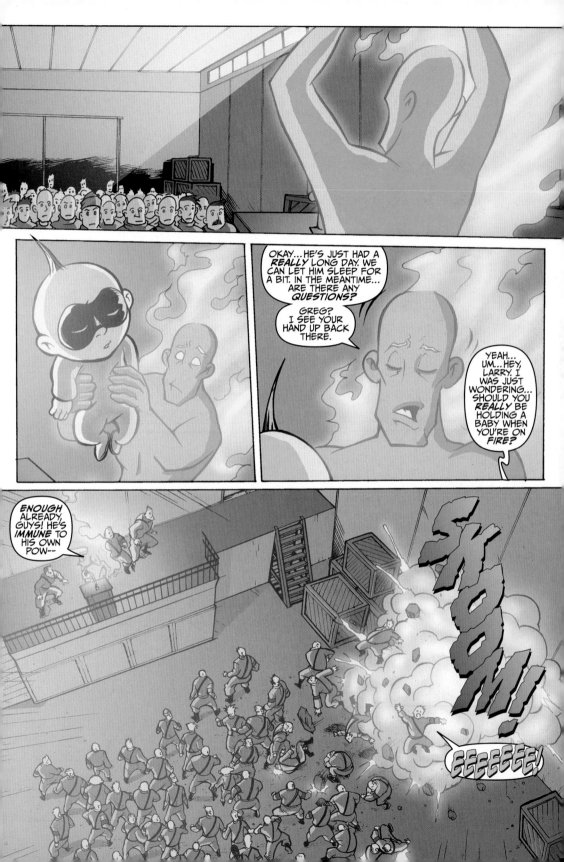

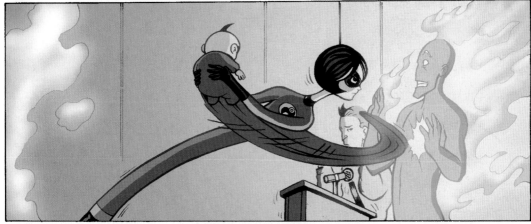

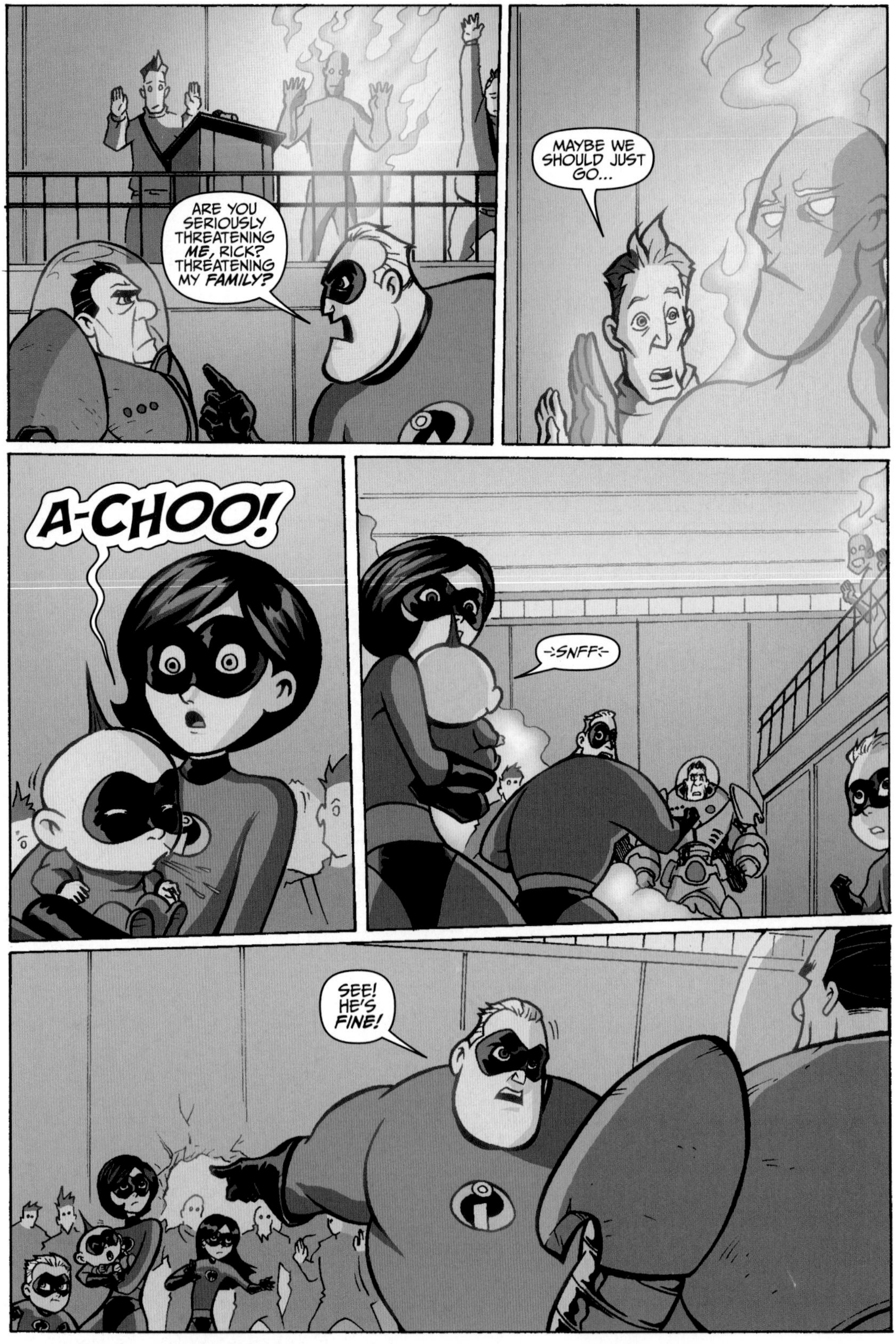
ARE YOU SERIOUSLY THREATENING *ME*, RICK? THREATENING MY *FAMILY?*
MAYBE WE SHOULD JUST GO...
A-CHOO!
-SNFF-
SEE! HE'S *FINE!*

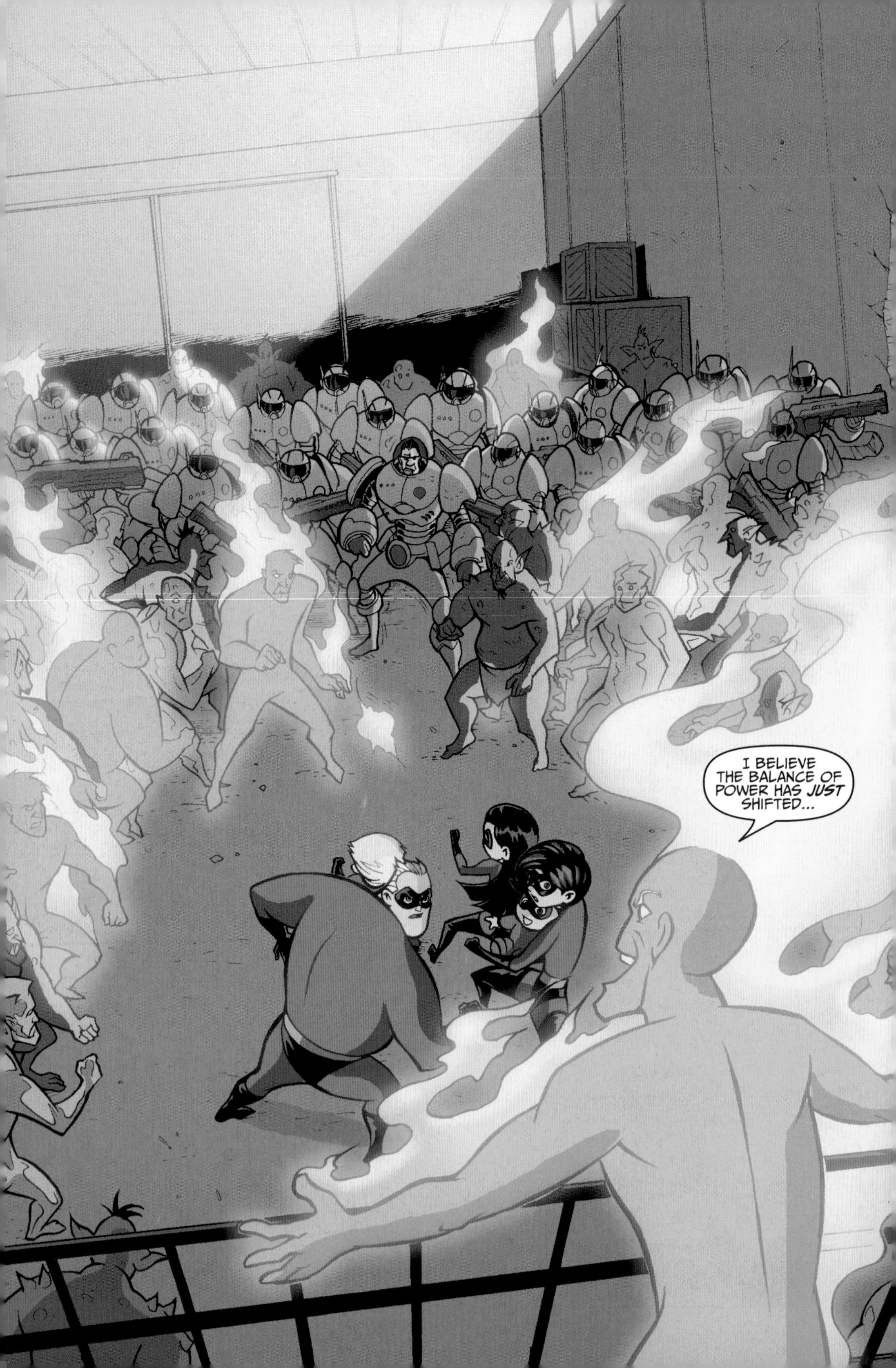
I BELIEVE THE BALANCE OF POWER HAS JUST SHIFTED...

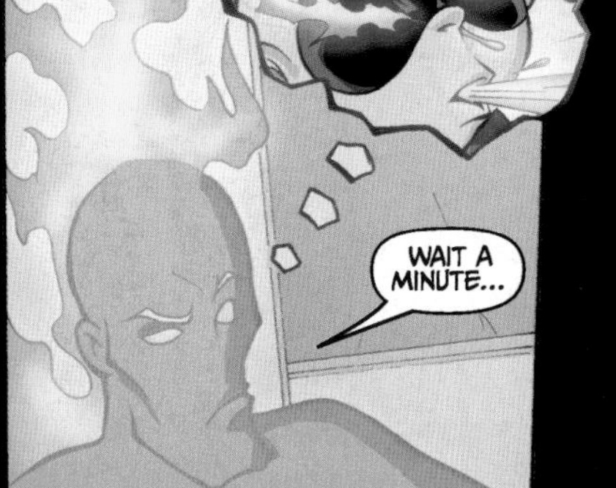
WAIT A MINUTE...

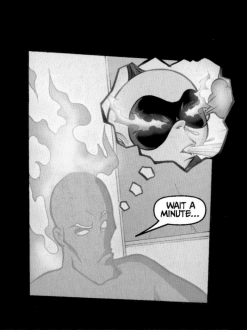

CHAPTER TWO

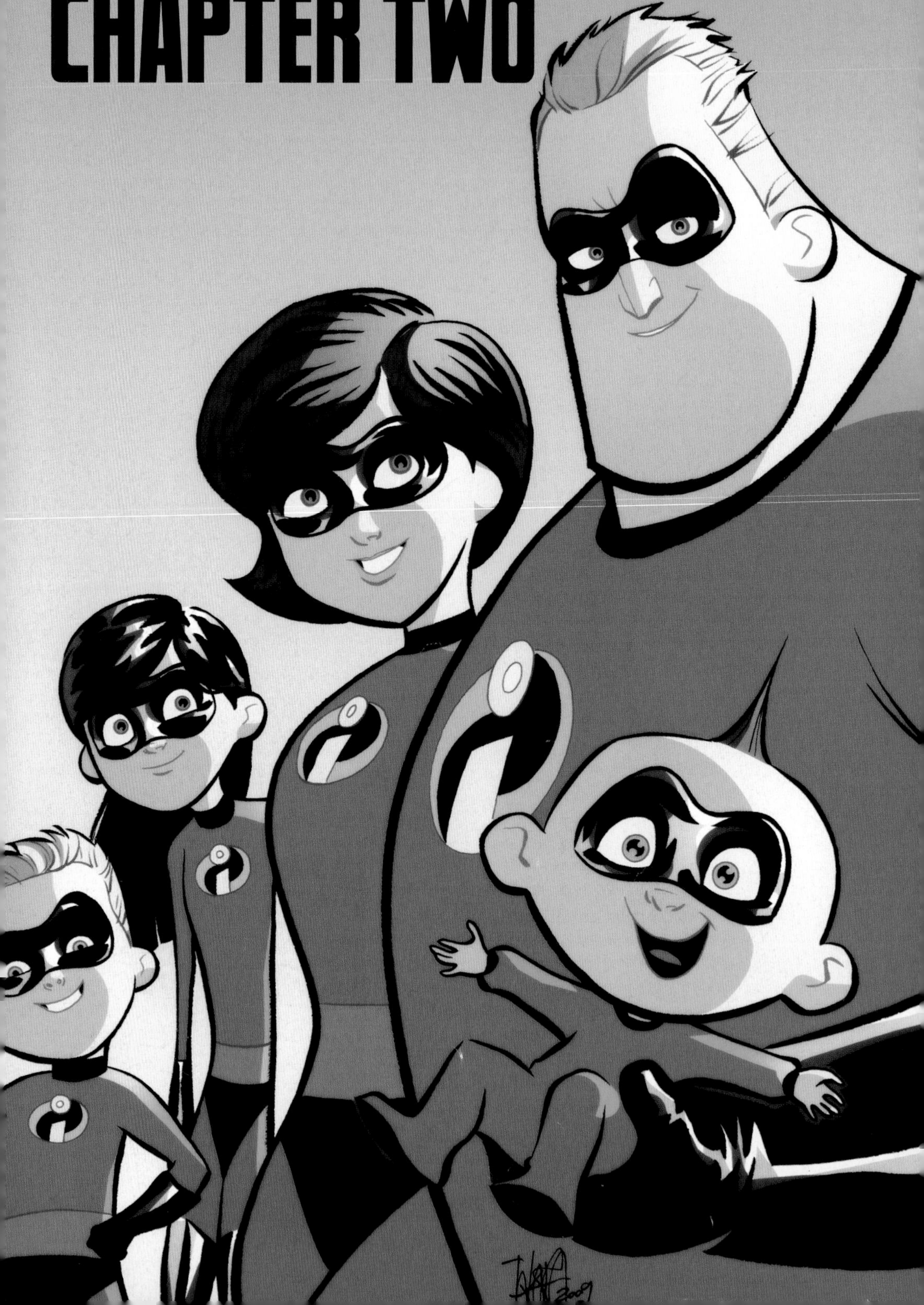

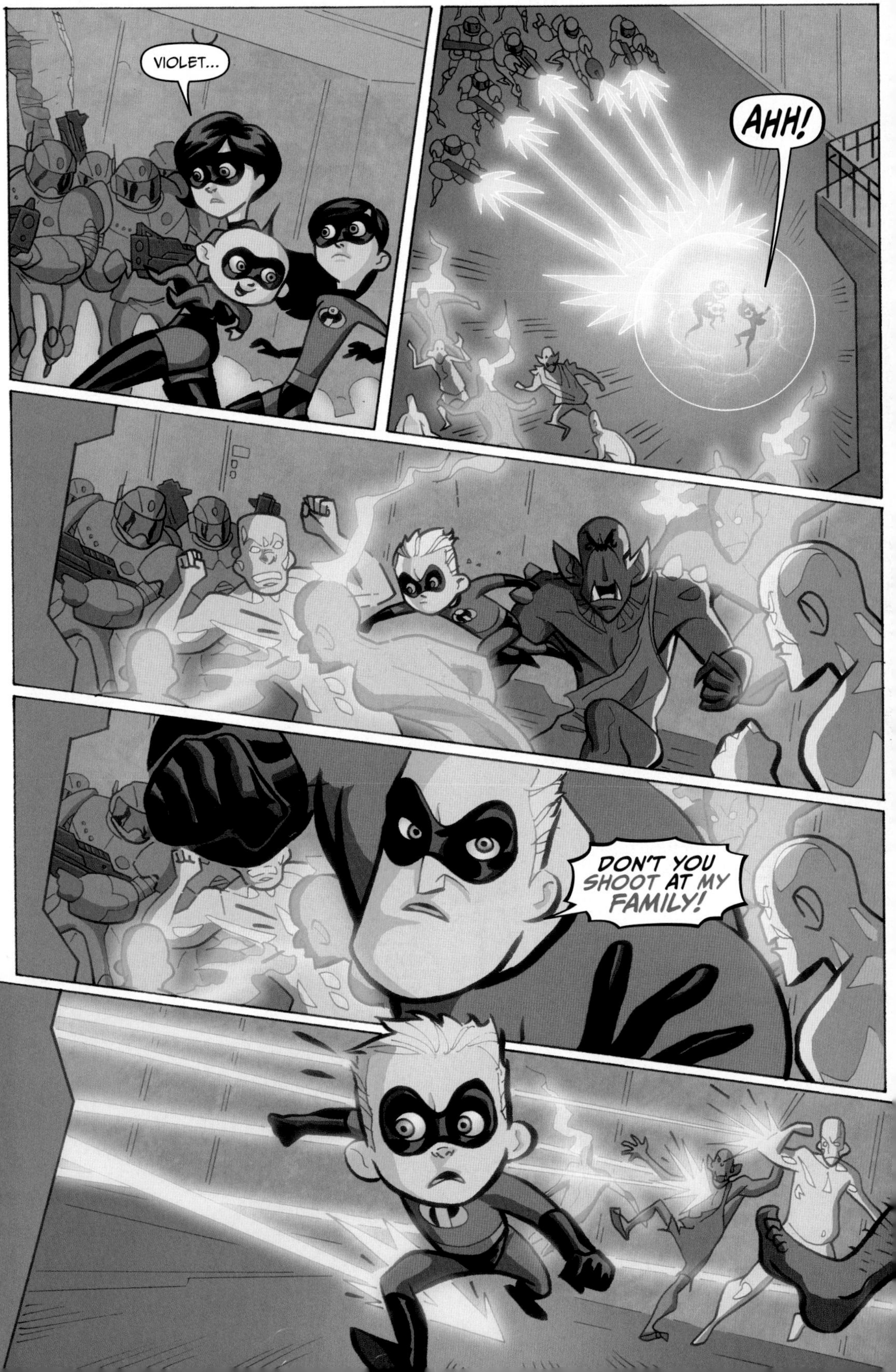
VIOLET...
AHH!
DON'T YOU SHOOT AT MY FAMILY!

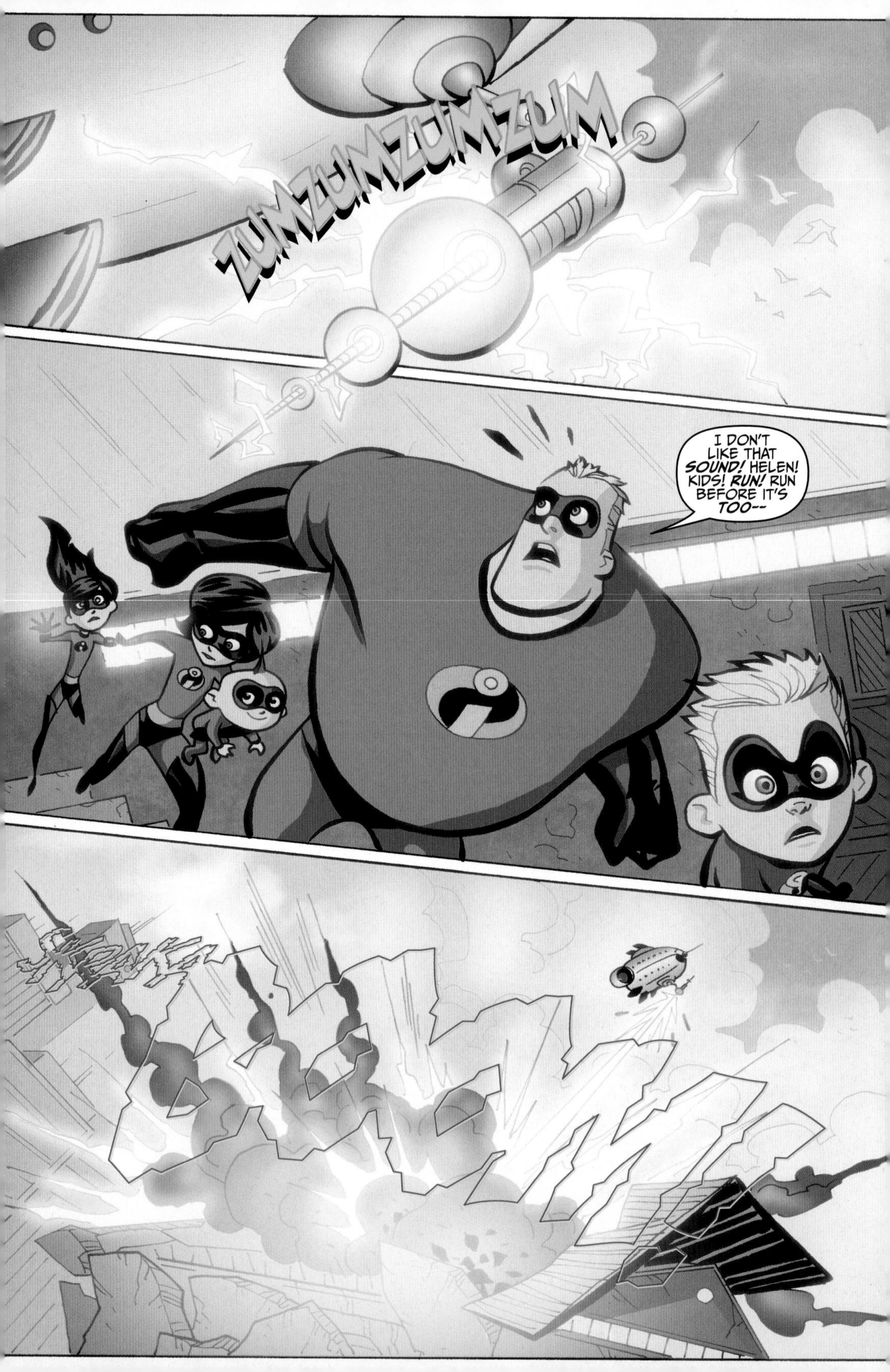
ZUMZUMZUMZUM
I DON'T LIKE THAT *SOUND!* HELEN! KIDS! *RUN!* RUN BEFORE IT'S *TOO--*

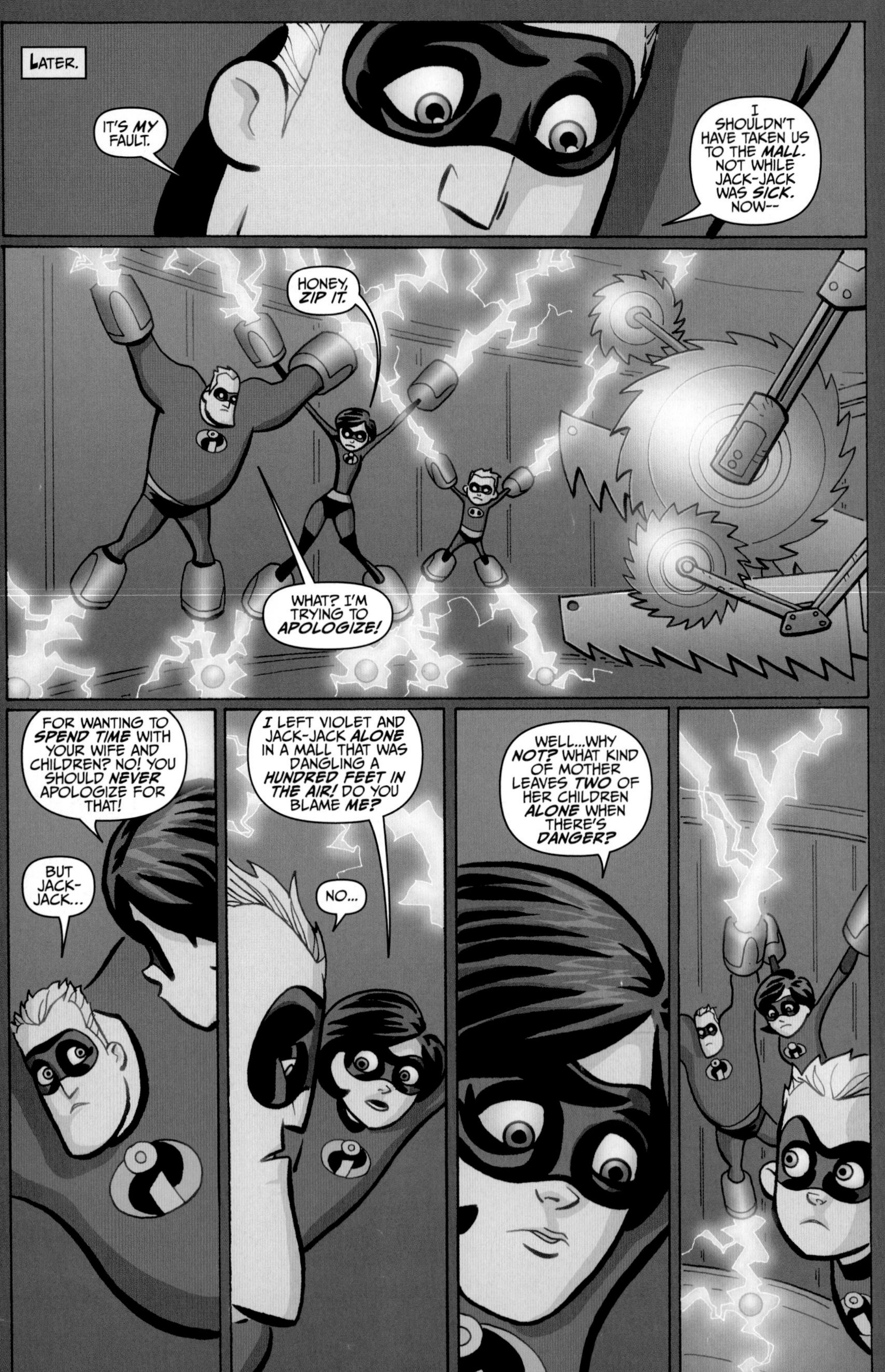
LATER.
IT'S MY FAULT.
I SHOULDN'T HAVE TAKEN US TO THE MALL. NOT WHILE JACK-JACK WAS SICK. NOW--
HONEY, ZIP IT.
WHAT? I'M TRYING TO APOLOGIZE!
FOR WANTING TO SPEND TIME WITH YOUR WIFE AND CHILDREN? NO! YOU SHOULD NEVER APOLOGIZE FOR THAT!
BUT JACK-JACK...
I LEFT VIOLET AND JACK-JACK ALONE IN A MALL THAT WAS DANGLING A HUNDRED FEET IN THE AIR! DO YOU BLAME ME?
NO...
WELL...WHY NOT? WHAT KIND OF MOTHER LEAVES TWO OF HER CHILDREN ALONE WHEN THERE'S DANGER?

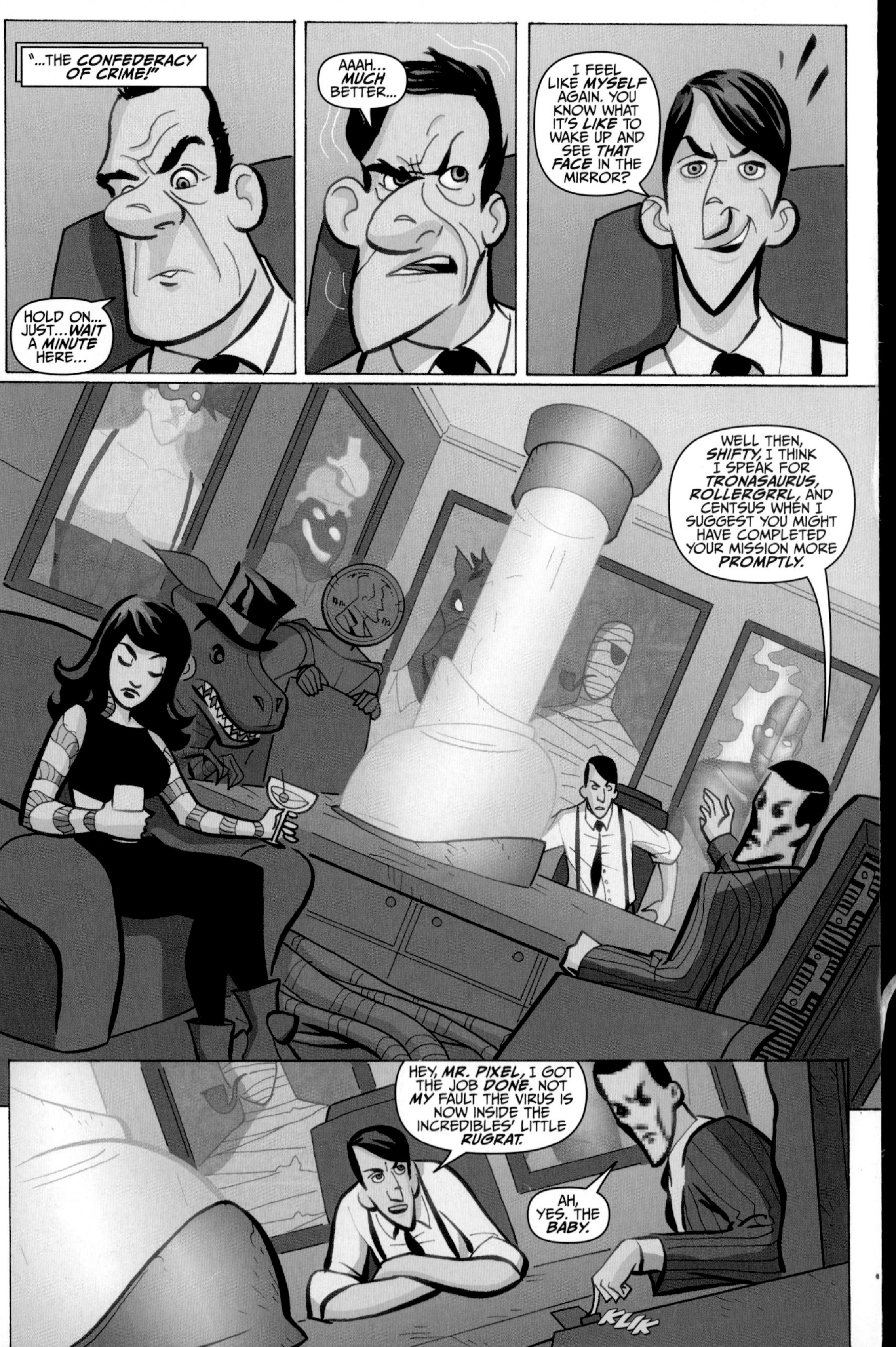

"...THE CONFEDERACY OF CRIME!"
HOLD ON... JUST...WAIT A MINUTE HERE...
AAAH... MUCH BETTER...
I FEEL LIKE MYSELF AGAIN. YOU KNOW WHAT IT'S LIKE TO WAKE UP AND SEE THAT FACE IN THE MIRROR?
WELL THEN, SHIFTY, I THINK I SPEAK FOR TRONASAURUS, ROLLERGRRL, AND CENTSUS WHEN I SUGGEST YOU MIGHT HAVE COMPLETED YOUR MISSION MORE PROMPTLY.
HEY, MR. PIXEL, I GOT THE JOB DONE. NOT MY FAULT THE VIRUS IS NOW INSIDE THE INCREDIBLES' LITTLE RUGRAT.
AH, YES. THE BABY.
KLIK

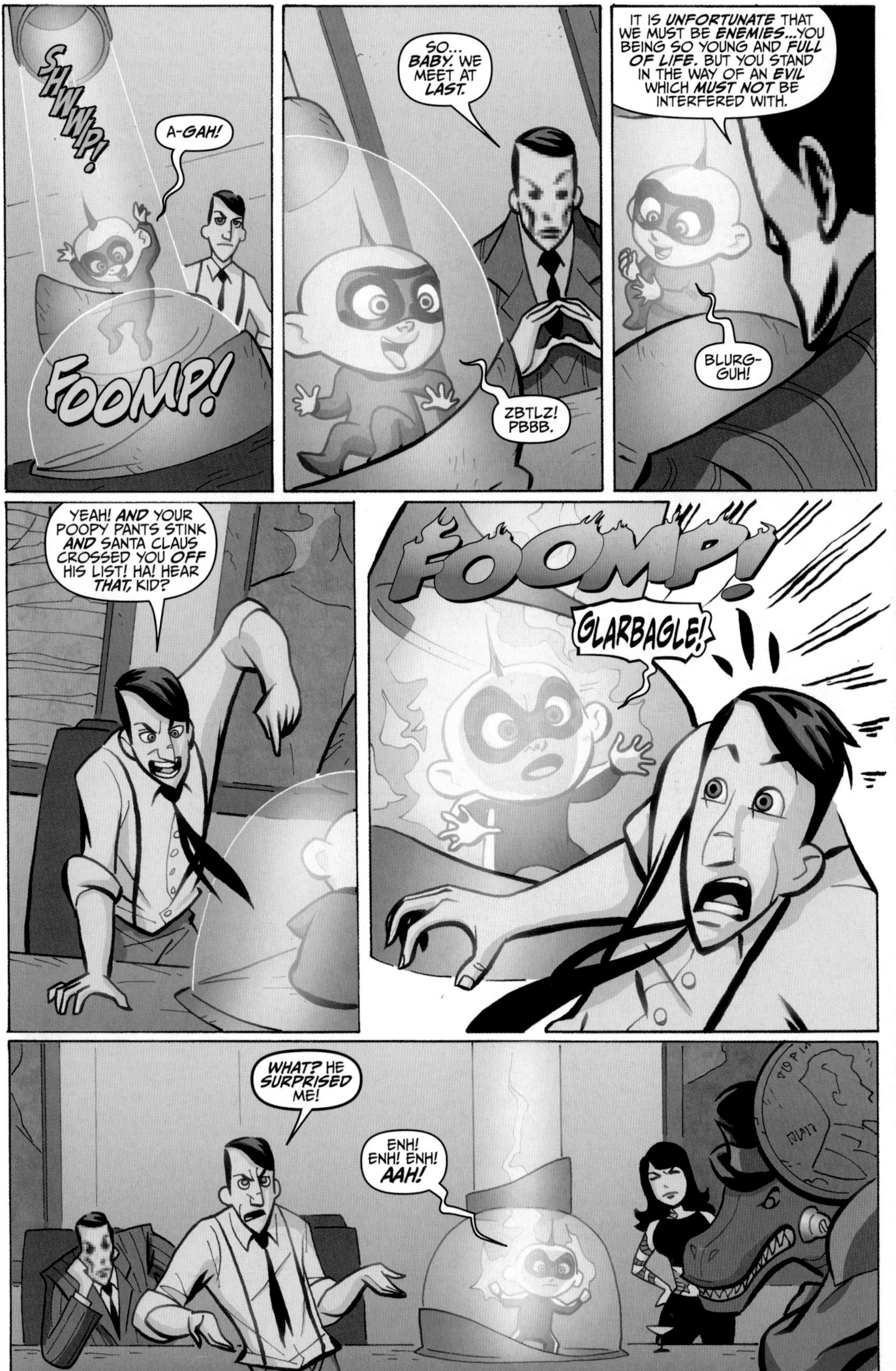
SHWWIP!
A-GAH!
FOOMP!
SO... BABY. WE MEET AT LAST.
ZBTLZ! PBBB.
IT IS UNFORTUNATE THAT WE MUST BE ENEMIES...YOU BEING SO YOUNG AND FULL OF LIFE. BUT YOU STAND IN THE WAY OF AN EVIL WHICH MUST NOT BE INTERFERED WITH.
BLURG-GUH!
YEAH! AND YOUR POOPY PANTS STINK AND SANTA CLAUS CROSSED YOU OFF HIS LIST! HA! HEAR THAT, KID?
FOOMP!
GLARBAGLE!
WHAT? HE SURPRISED ME!
ENH! ENH! ENH! AAH!

DO NOT TAUNT THE BABY.

SHHWWP!

FOOMP!

FINE, WHATEVER.

GHHEEE!

YOU ISOLATED *ALL* THE INDIVIDUALS INFECTED BY THE CHILD, AS *INSTRUCTED*?

YEAH... A BUNCH OF GOOFY HENCHMEN WHO *THOUGHT* THEY'D BE THE NEXT *BIG THING.* I GOT 'EM LOCKED UP.

BUT *BETTER* THAN THAT...

KLIK

OH, NO!

WHAT?

THEM? YOU BROUGHT THEM *HERE?* ONTO *OUR* SKYSHIP?

YOU-FOOL-YOU- HAVE-ENDANGERED... ENDANGERED... endangeredddd...

KLONK!

OH, COME ON...DID *NO ONE* THINK TO RECHARGE TRONASAURUS LAST NIGHT?

SO WHAT WAS I *SUPPOSED* TO DO? LEAVE THE INCREDIBLES FREE TO HUNT US DOWN? I HAD *NO CHOICE!*

TAUNTING BABIES? TAKING *CAPTIVES?* YOUR TIME *UNDERCOVER* HAS MADE YOU *SOFT,* SHIFTY.

THIS IS WHAT WE DO WITH OUR *ENEMIES!*

KLIK

WHREEEEEEEEE

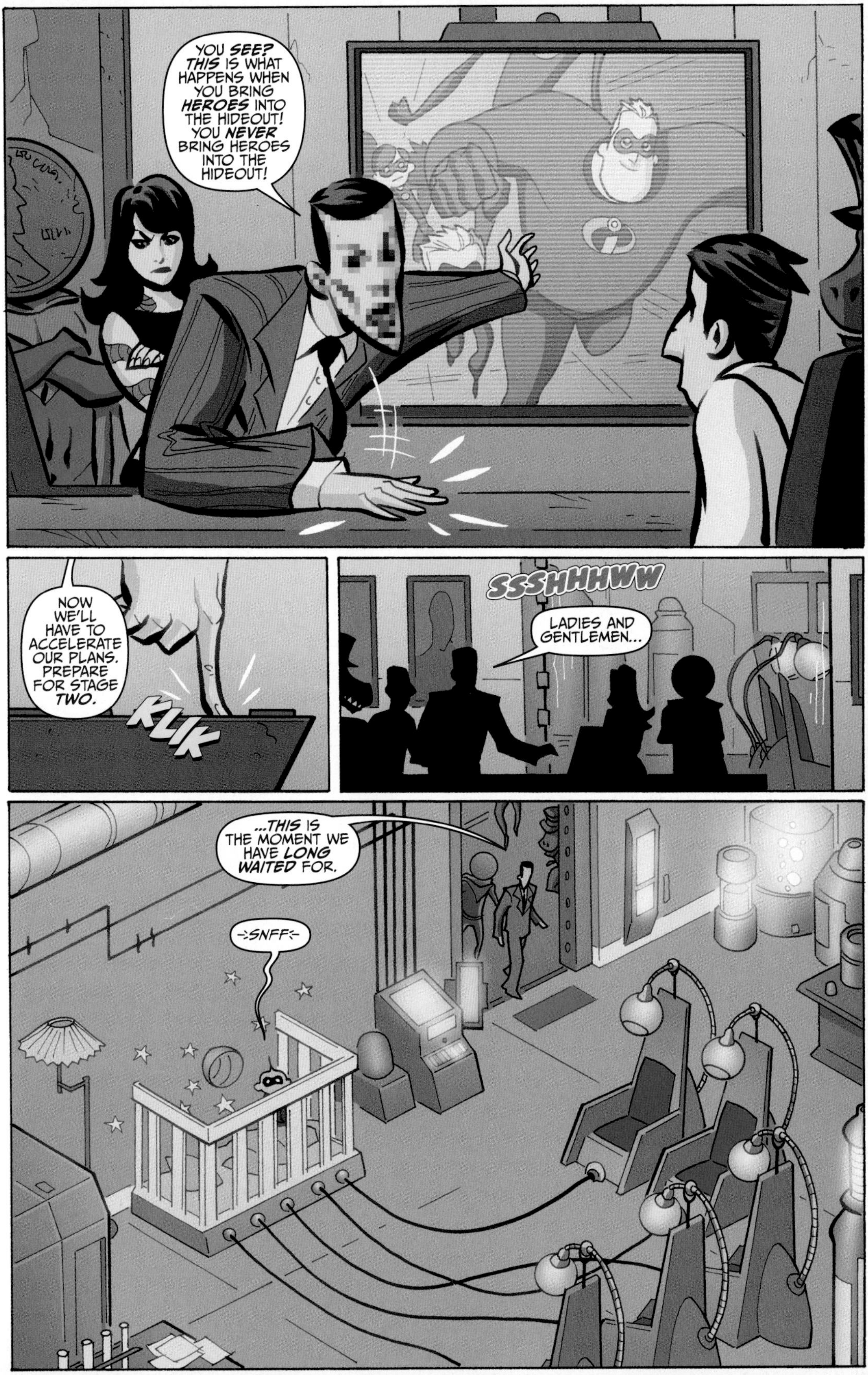
YOU **SEE? THIS** IS WHAT HAPPENS WHEN YOU BRING **HEROES** INTO THE HIDEOUT! YOU **NEVER** BRING HEROES INTO THE HIDEOUT!
NOW WE'LL HAVE TO ACCELERATE OUR PLANS. PREPARE FOR STAGE **TWO.**
KLIK
SSSHHHWW
LADIES AND GENTLEMEN...
...**THIS** IS THE MOMENT WE HAVE **LONG WAITED** FOR.
-SNFF-

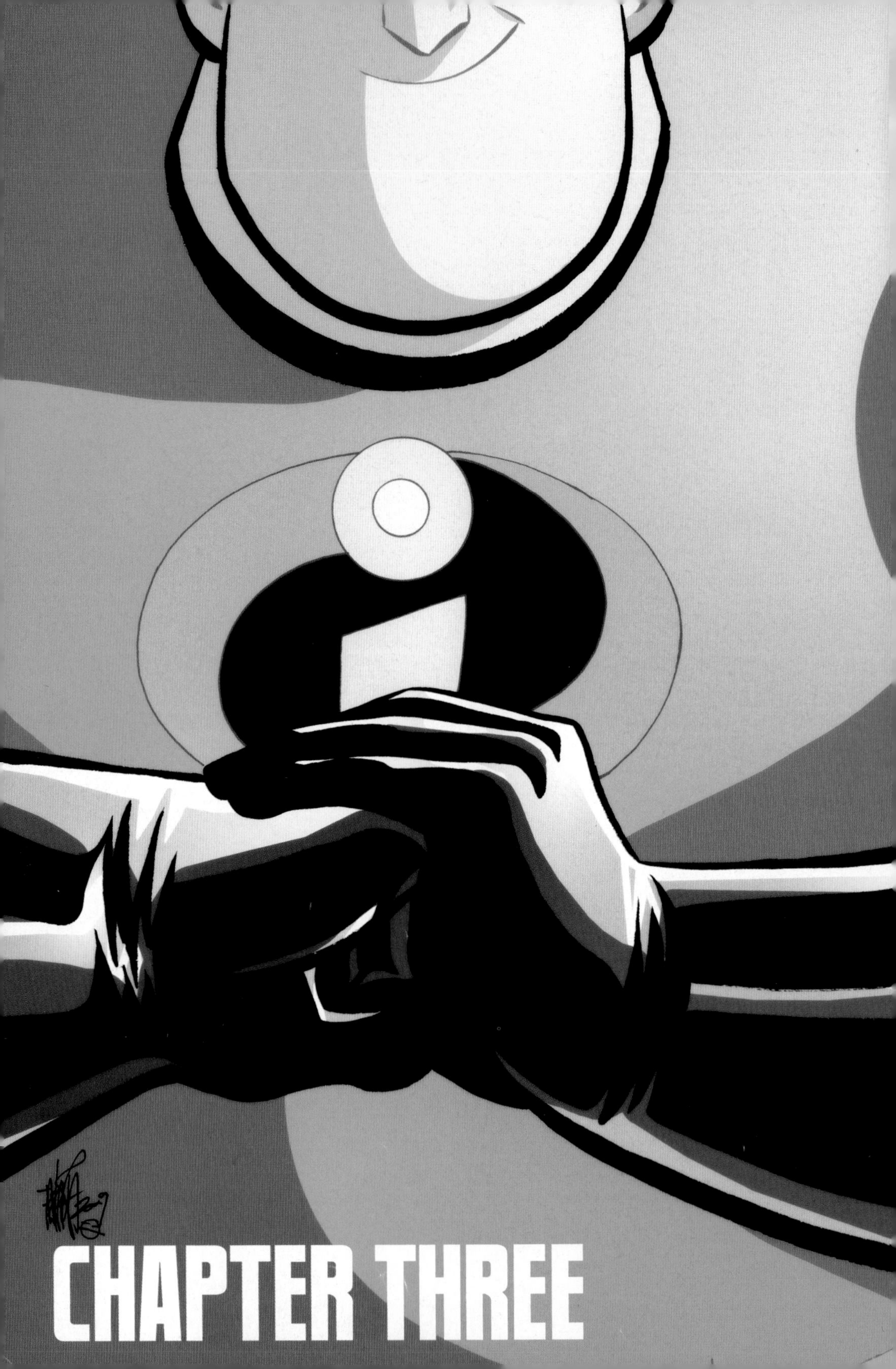

CHAPTER THREE

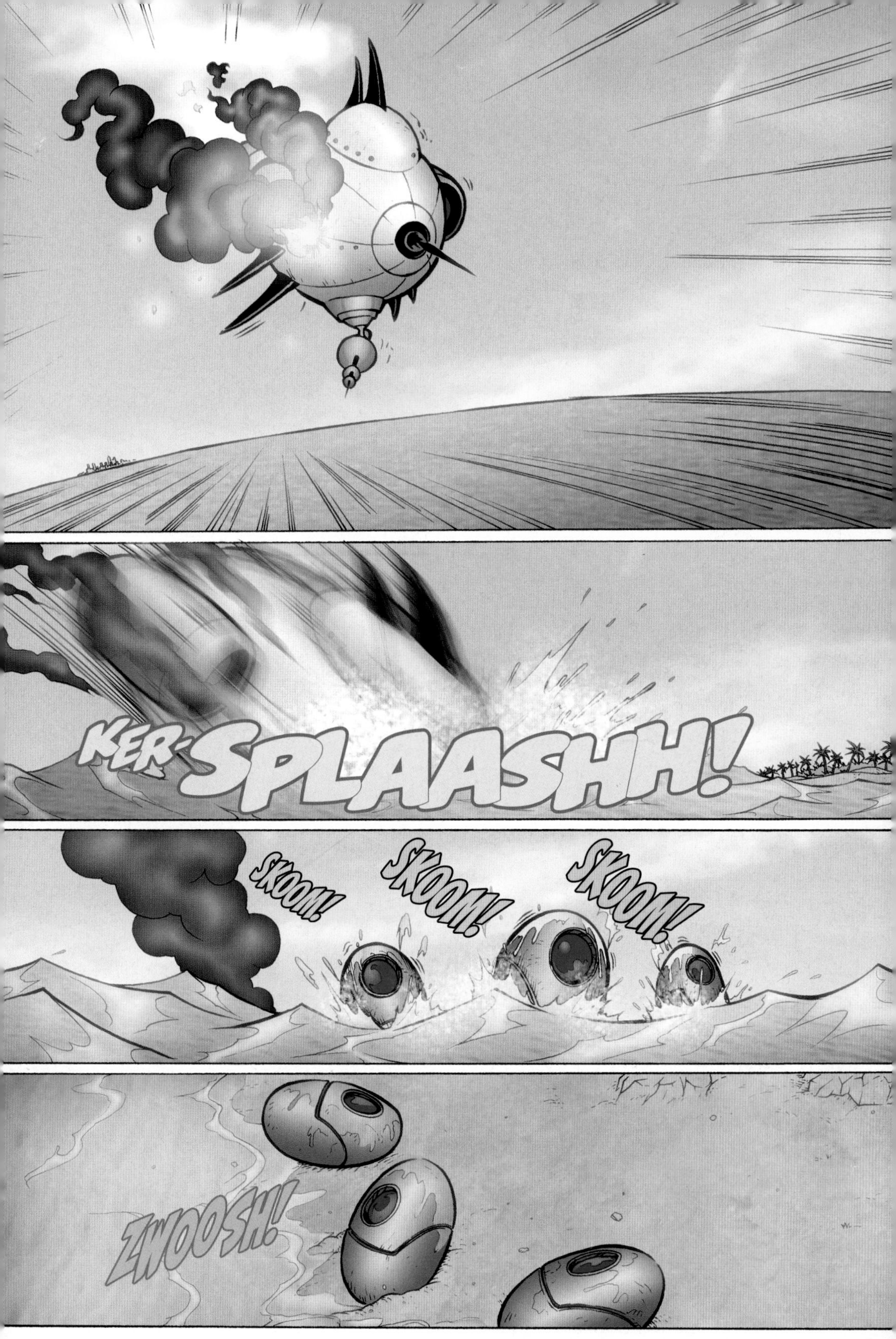
KER-SPLAASHH!
SKOOM!
SKOOM!
SKOOM!
ZWOOSH!

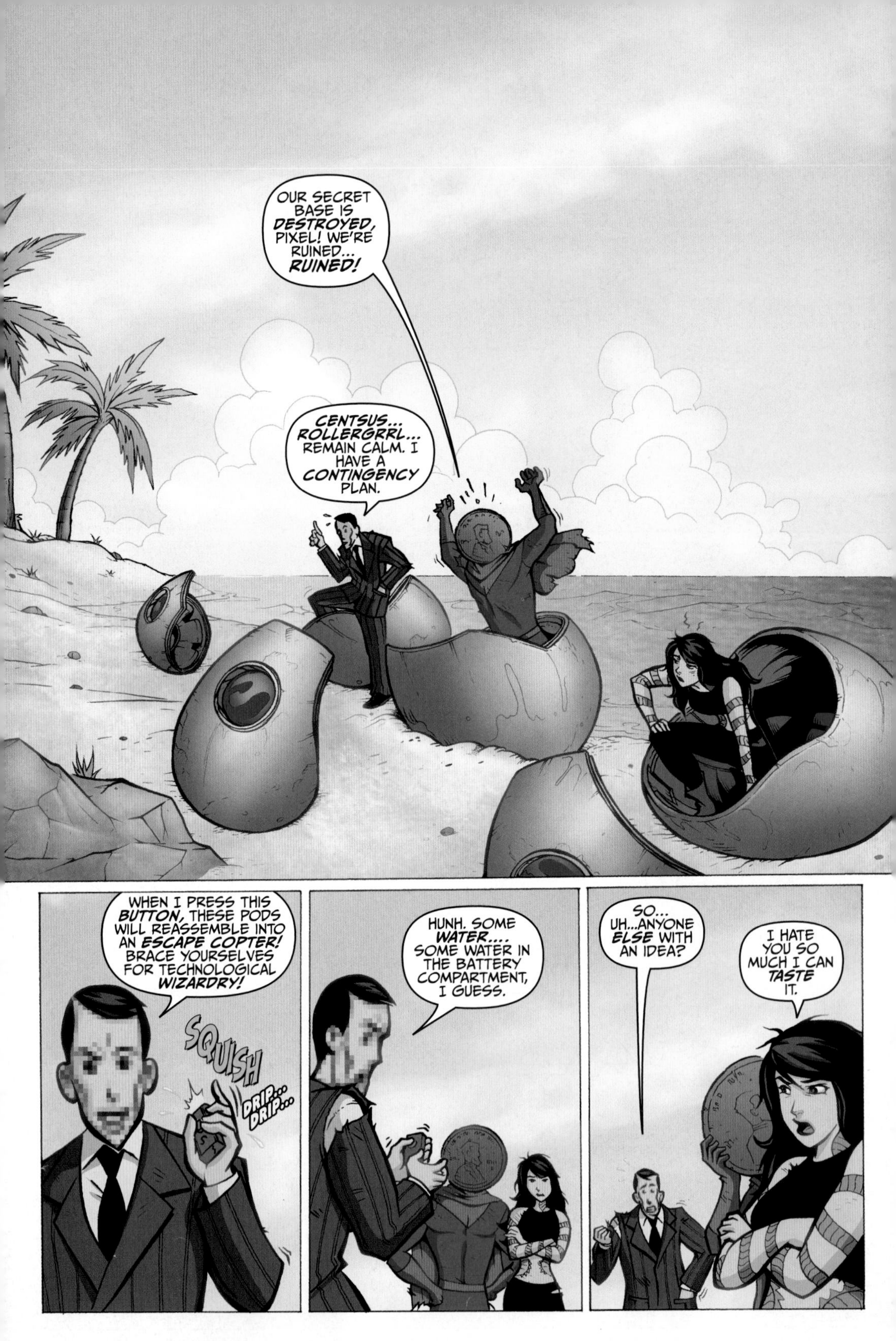
OUR SECRET BASE IS DESTROYED, PIXEL! WE'RE RUINED... RUINED!
CENTSUS... ROLLERGRRL... REMAIN CALM. I HAVE A CONTINGENCY PLAN.
WHEN I PRESS THIS BUTTON, THESE PODS WILL REASSEMBLE INTO AN ESCAPE COPTER! BRACE YOURSELVES FOR TECHNOLOGICAL WIZARDRY!
SQUISH
DRIP... DRIP...
HUNH. SOME WATER.... SOME WATER IN THE BATTERY COMPARTMENT, I GUESS.
SO... UH...ANYONE ELSE WITH AN IDEA?
I HATE YOU SO MUCH I CAN TASTE IT.

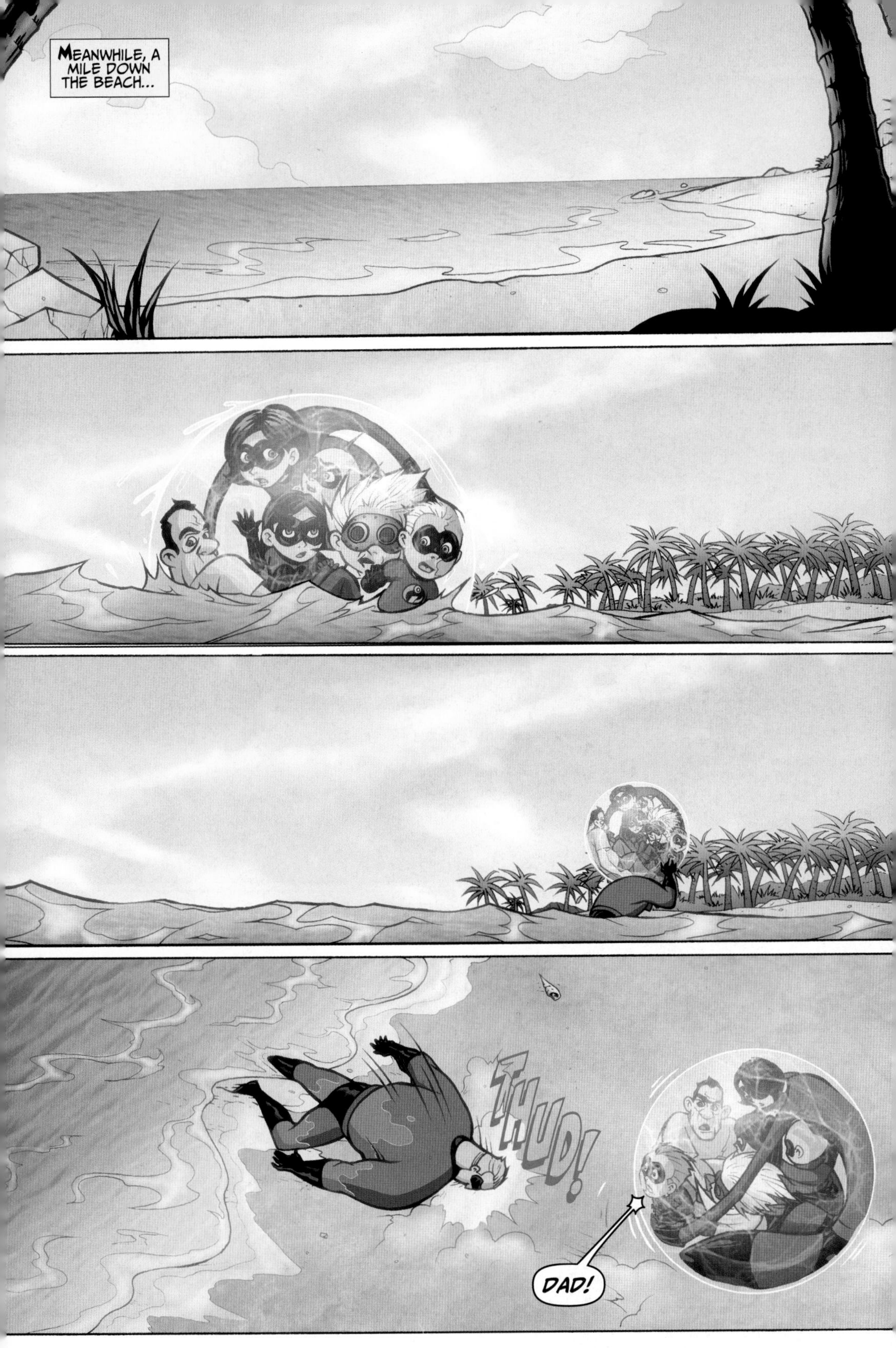
MEANWHILE, A MILE DOWN THE BEACH...
THUD!
DAD!

ZOOM!

ZOOM!

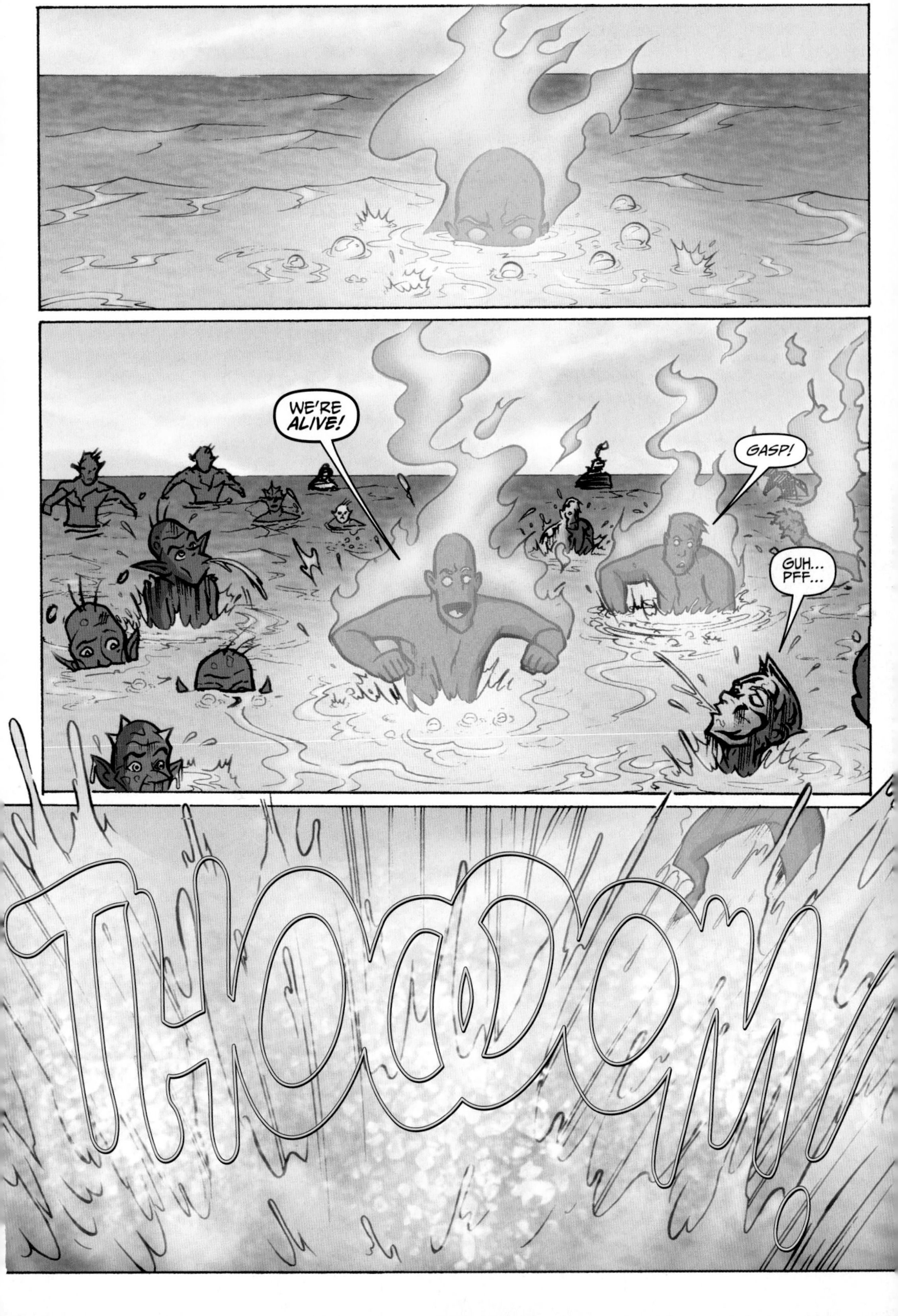
WE'RE ALIVE!
GASP!
GUH... PFF...
THOOOOM!

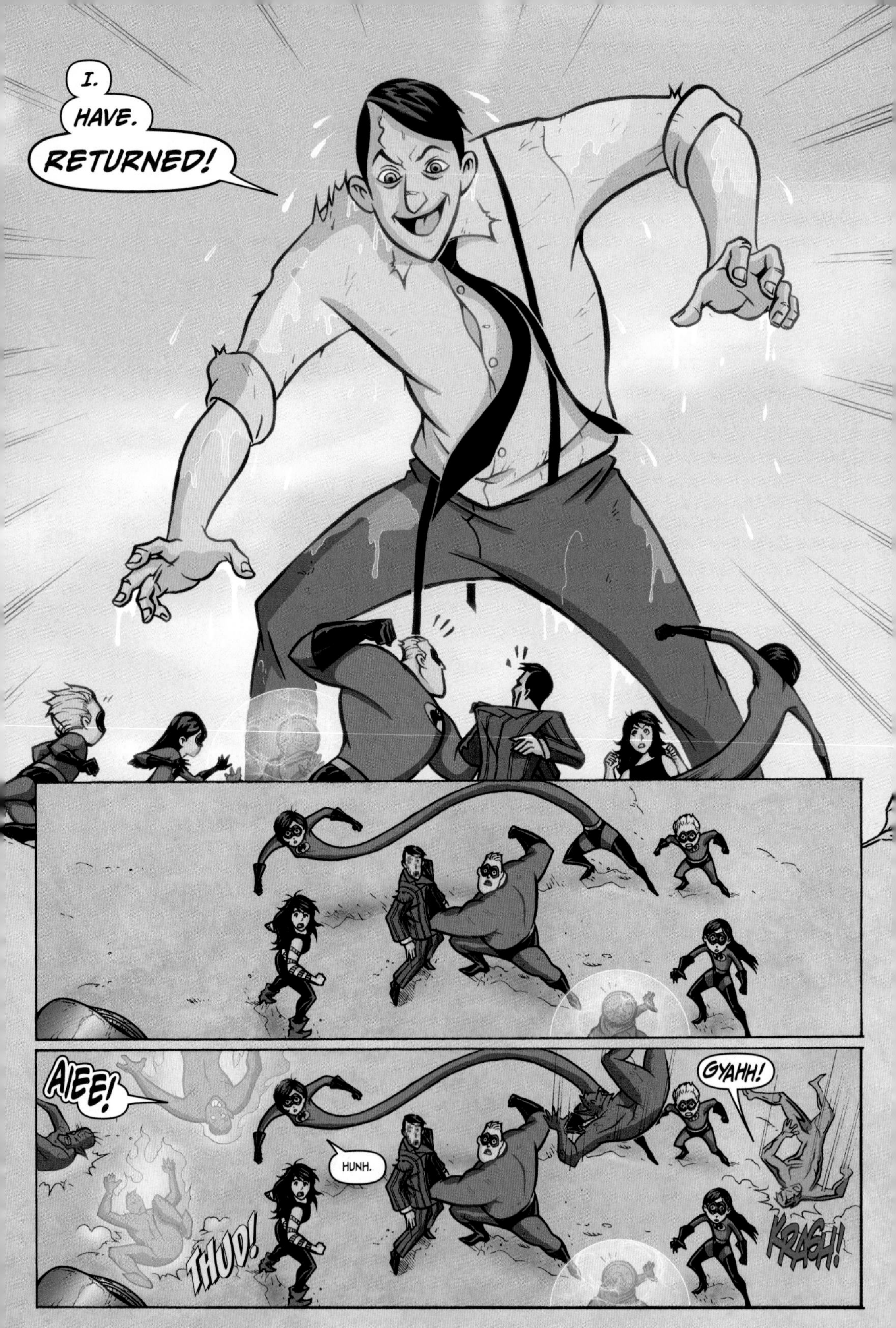
I.
HAVE.
RETURNED!
AIEE!
HUNH.
GYAHH!
THUD!
KRASH!

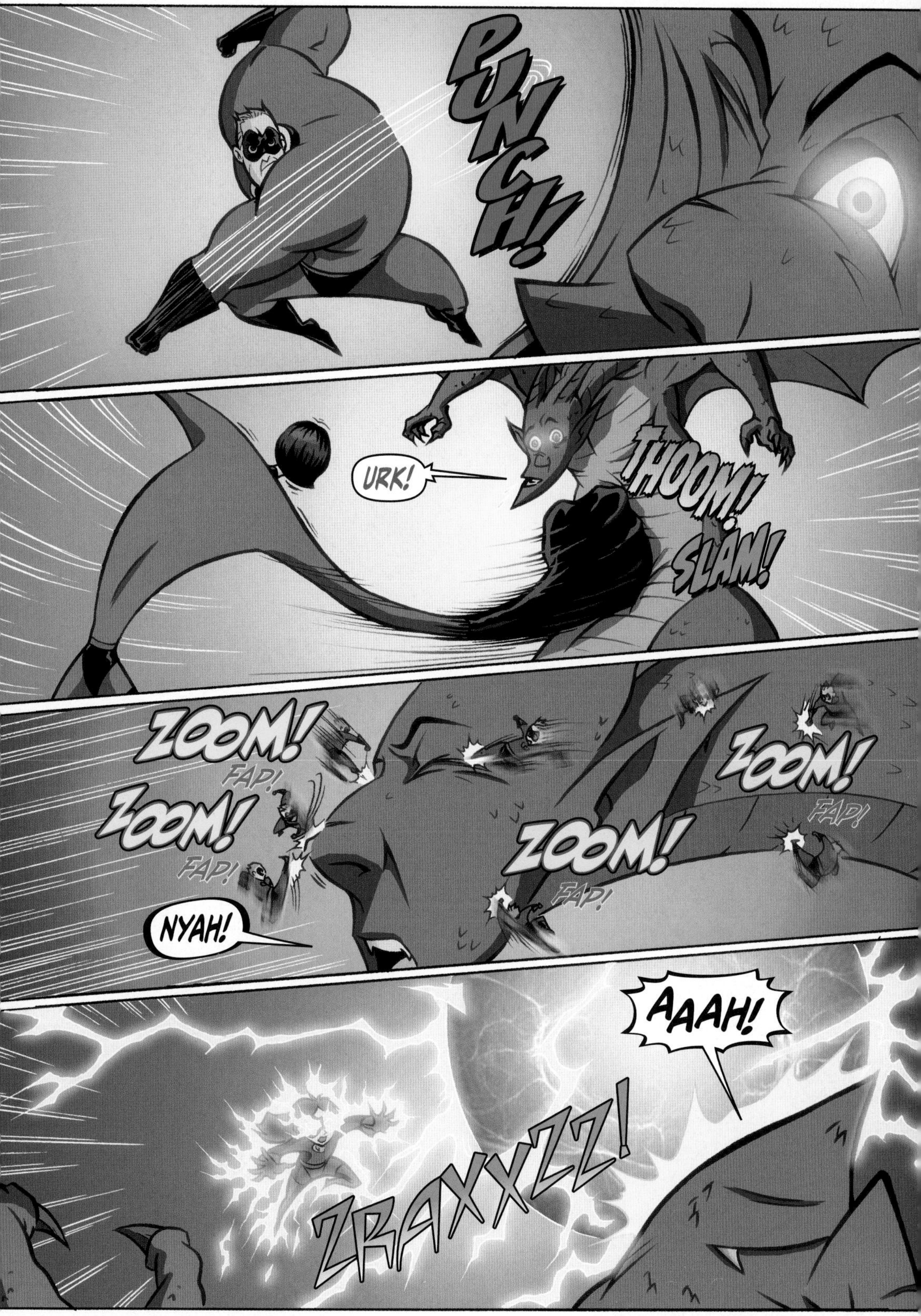
PUNCH!
URK!
THOOM!
SLAM!
ZOOM!
FAP!
ZOOM!
FAP!
NYAH!
ZOOM!
FAP!
ZOOM!
FAP!
AAAH!
ZRAXXZZ!

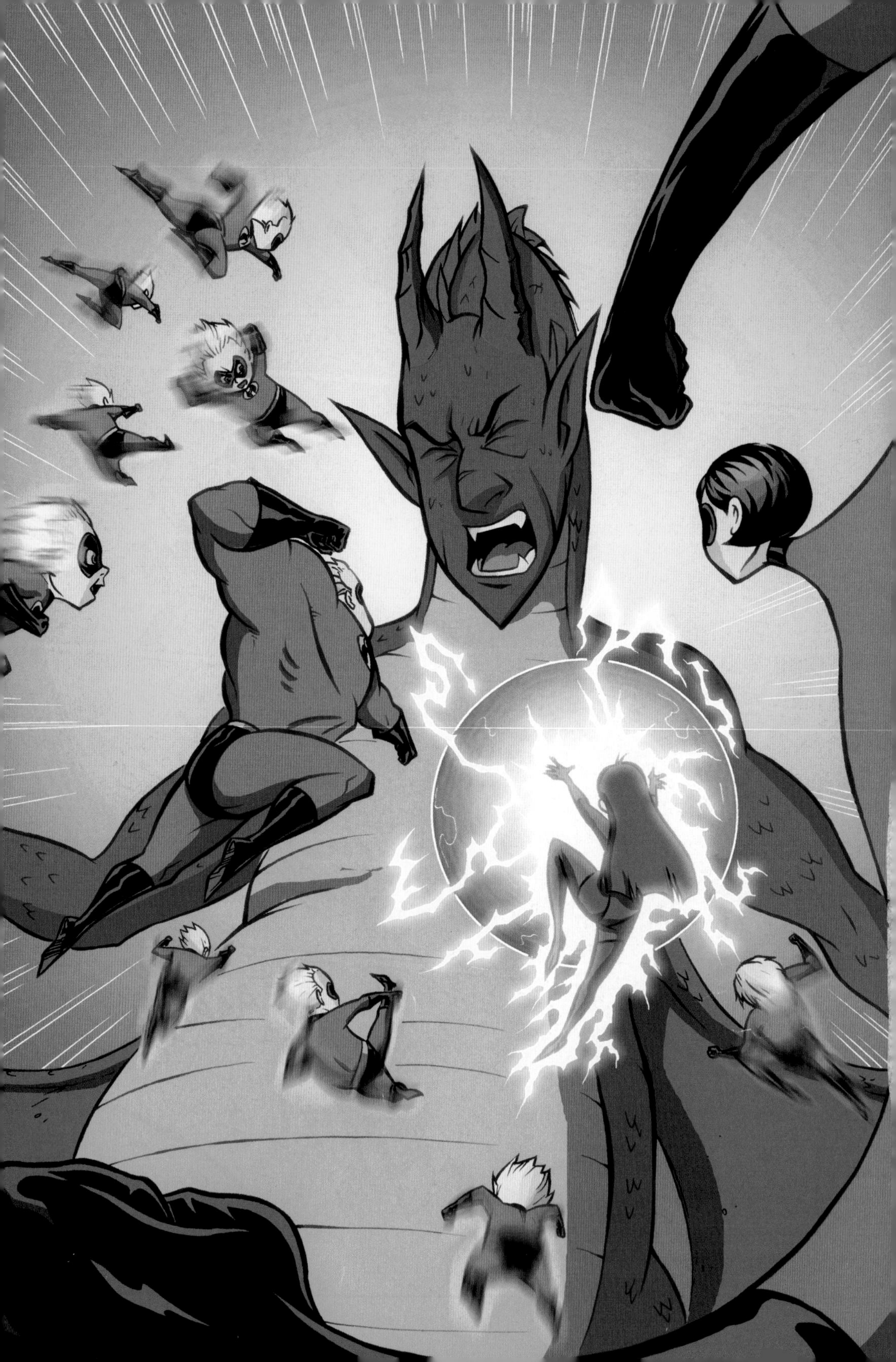

COVER GALLERY

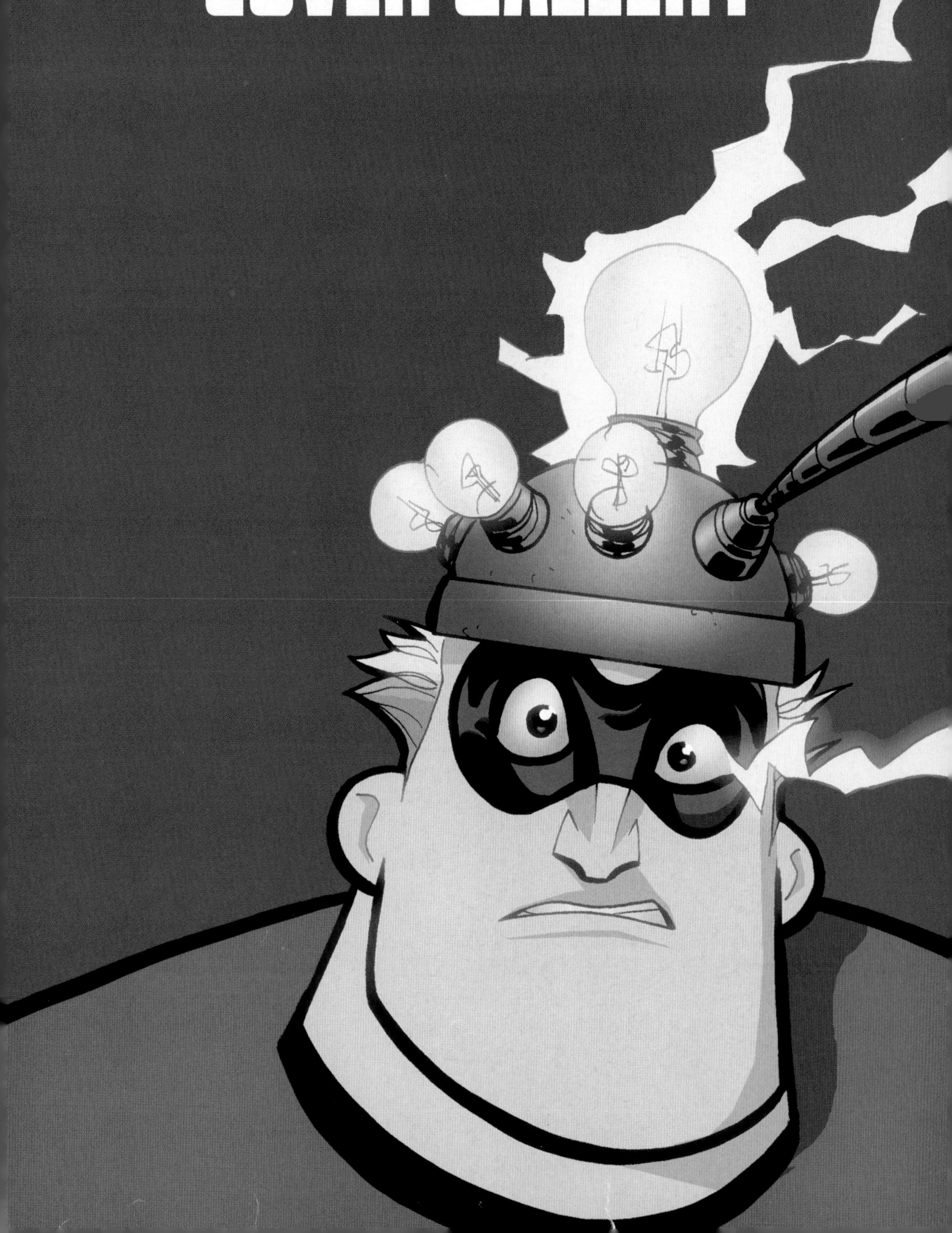

ULTIMATE COMICS EXCLUSIVE: TOMMY LEE EDWARDS

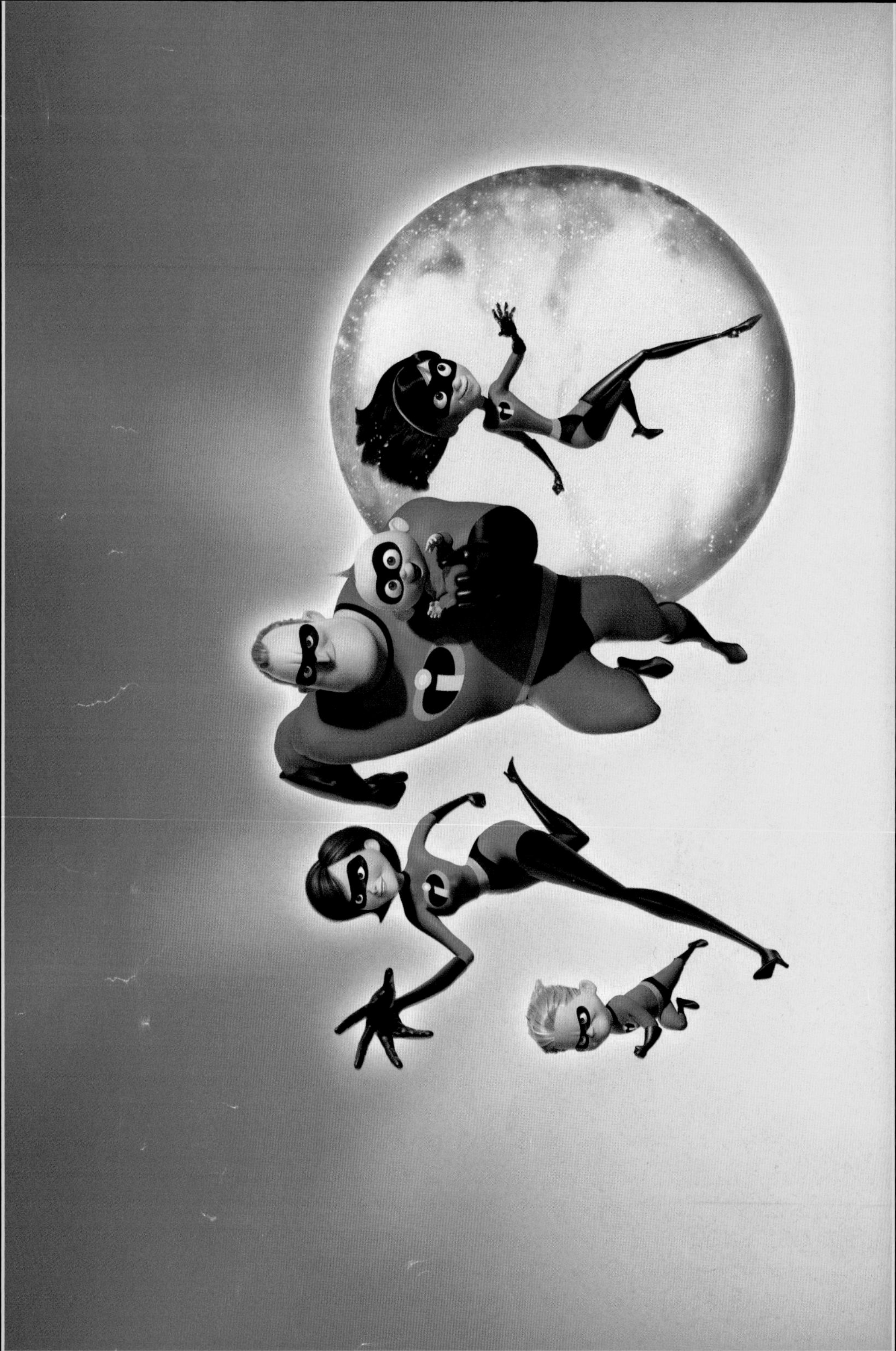

LBCC EXCLUSIVE: PHOTO COVER

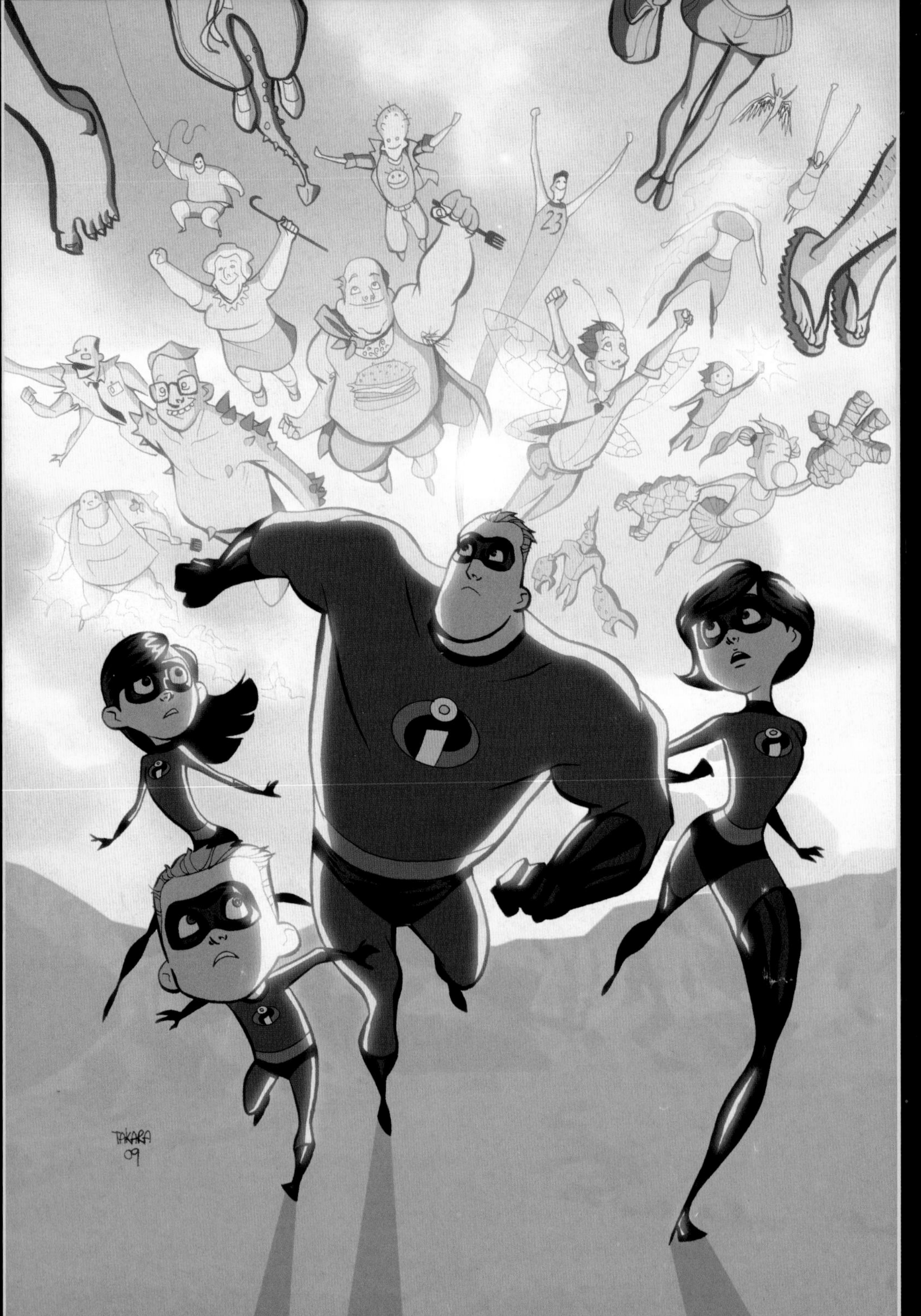
TAKARA
09

COVER 2A: MARCIO TAKARA

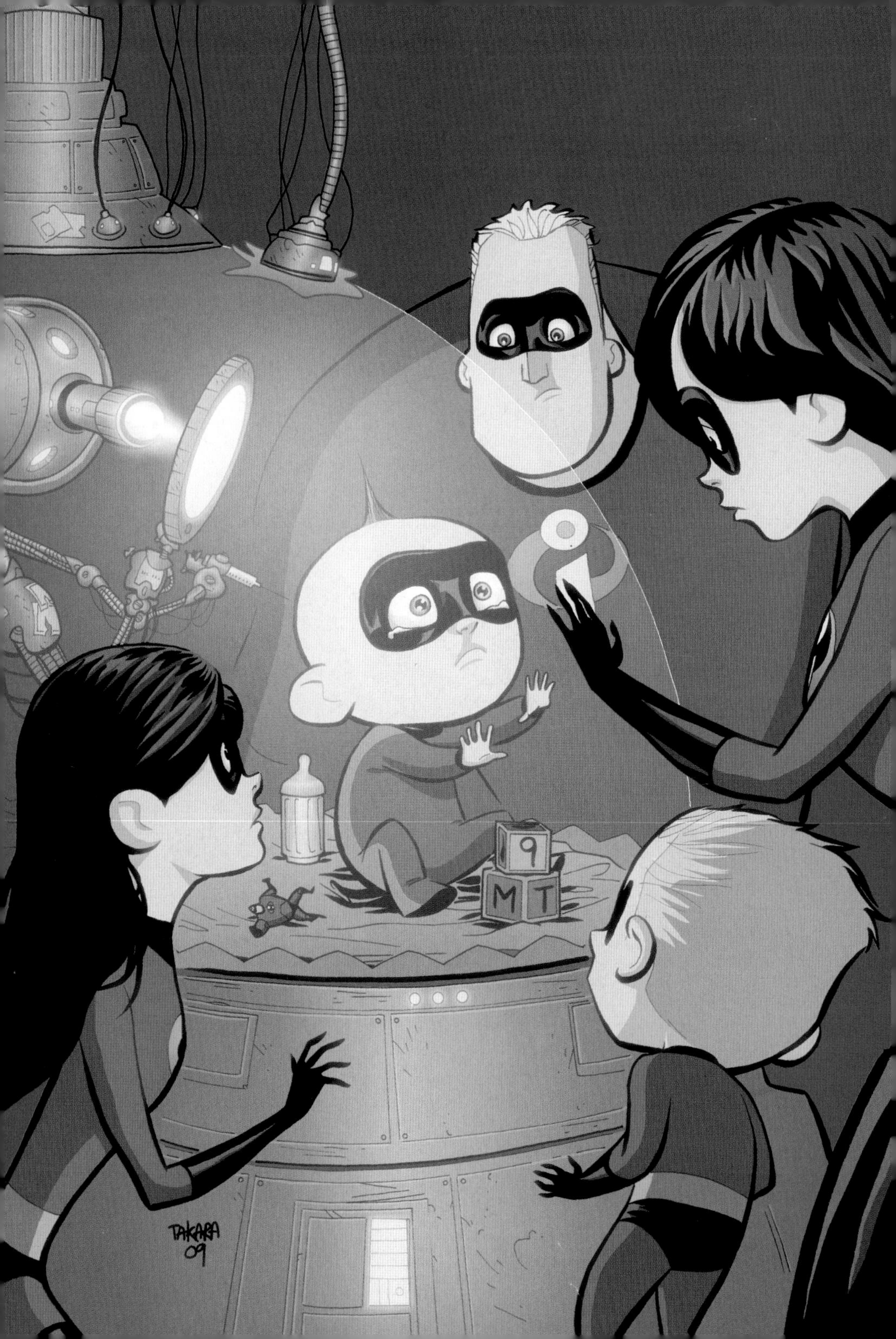
TAKARA
09

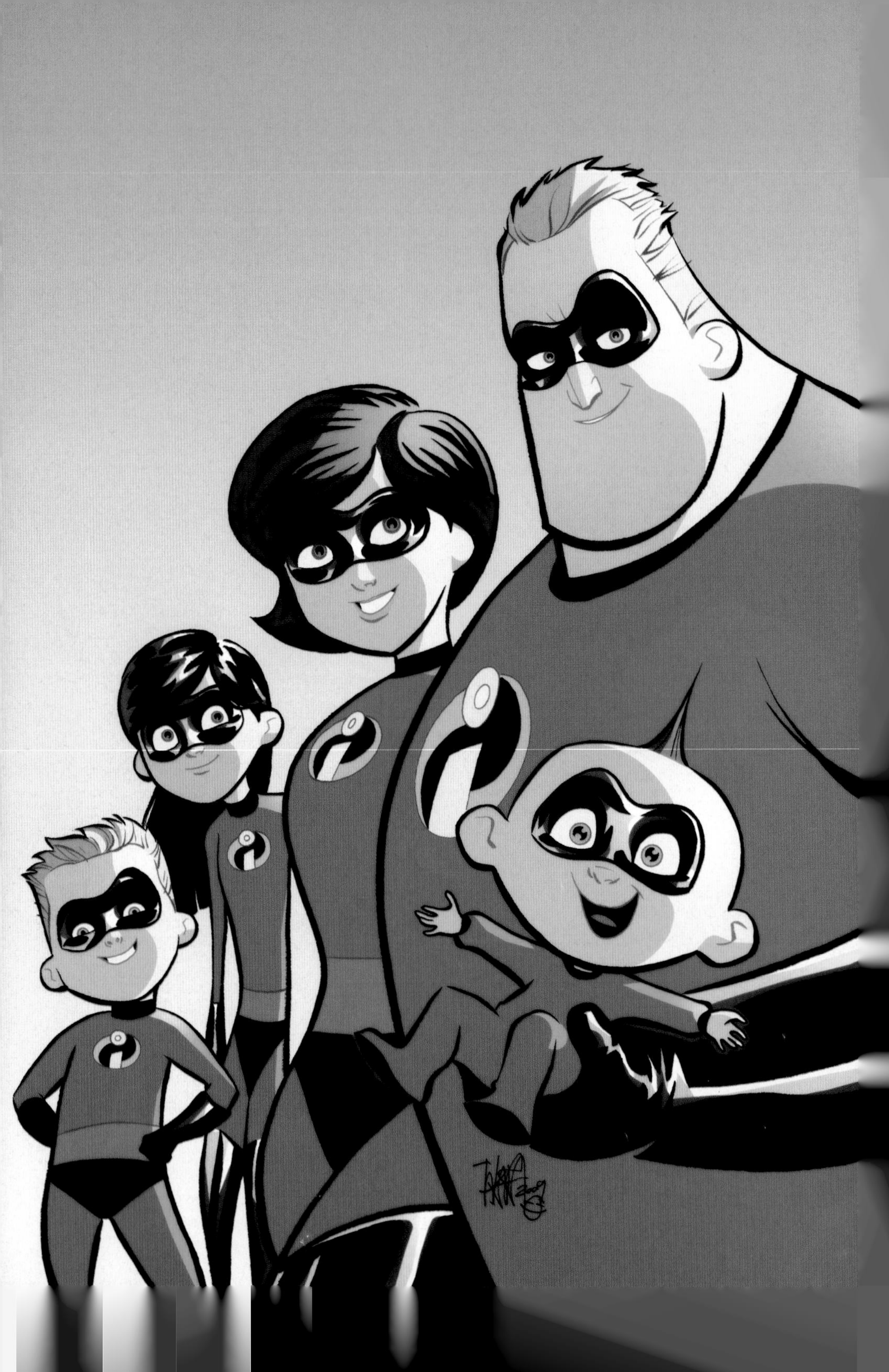

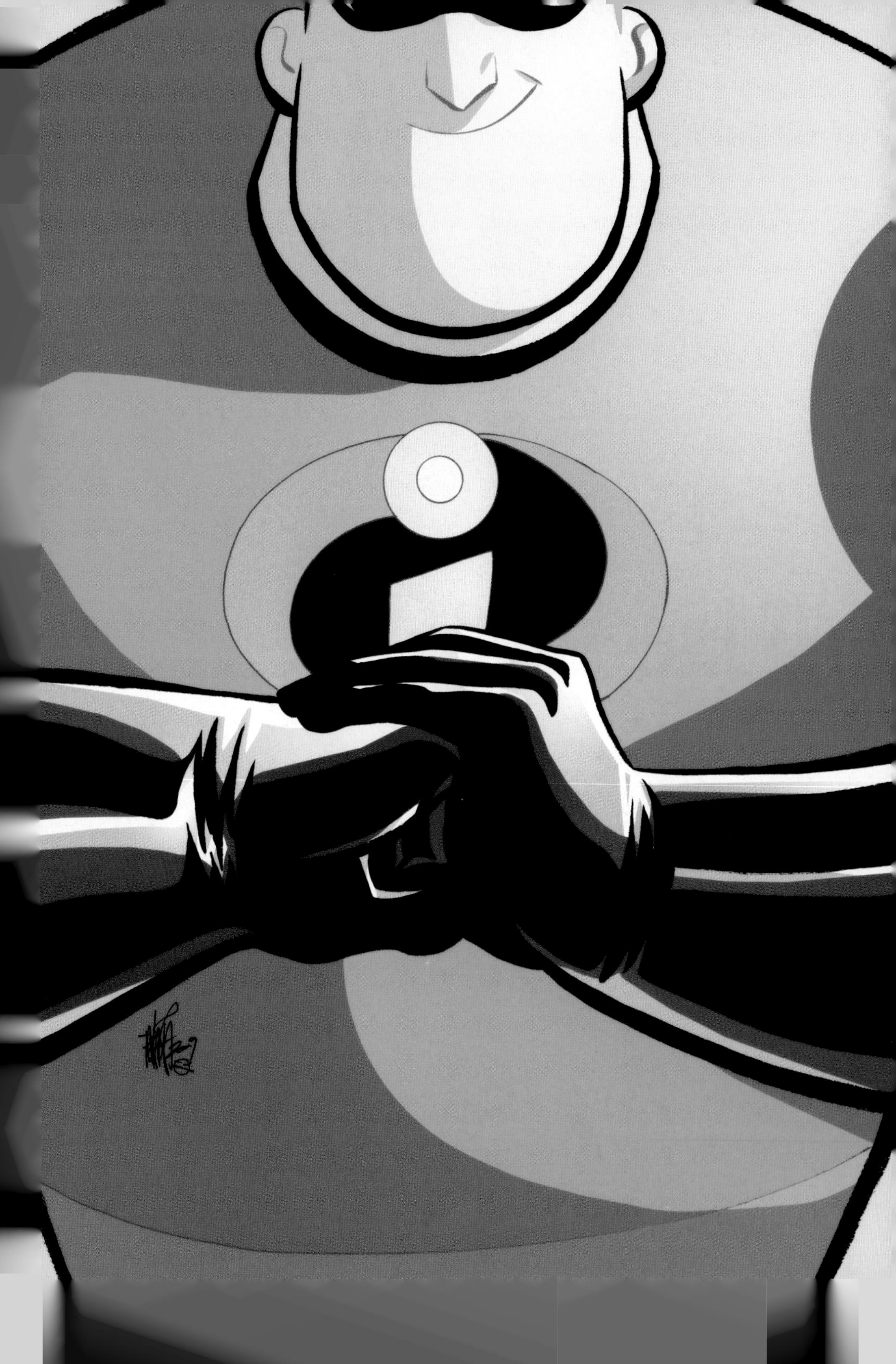

THE MUPPET SHOW COMIC BOOK: MEET THE MUPPETS

SC $9.99 ISBN 9781934506851
HC $24.99 ISBN 9781608865277

CARS: THE ROOKIE

SC $9.99 ISBN 9781934506844
HC $24.99 ISBN 9781608865222

FINDING NEMO: REEF RESCUE

SC $9.99 ISBN 9781934506882
HC $24.99 ISBN 9781608865246

**THE MUPPET SHOW COMIC BOOK:
THE TREASURE OF PEG-LEG WILSON**

SC $9.99 ISBN 9781608865048
HC $24.99 ISBN 9781608865307

MUPPET ROBIN HOOD

SC $9.99 ISBN 9781934506790
HC $24.99 ISBN 9781608865260

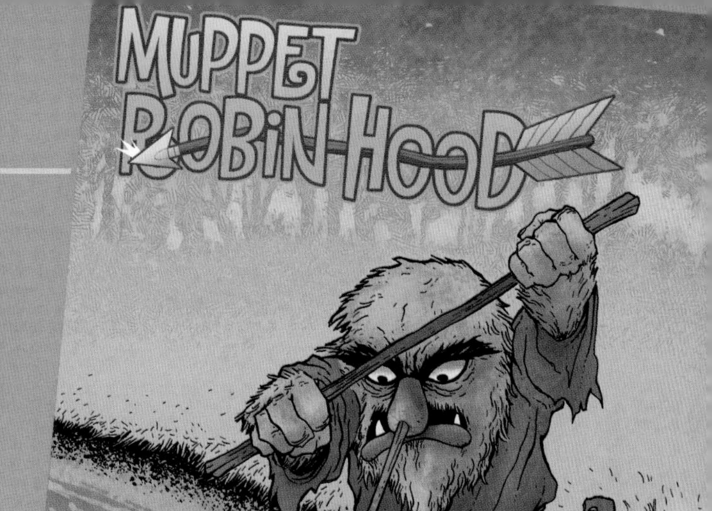
MUPPET
ROBIN HOOD

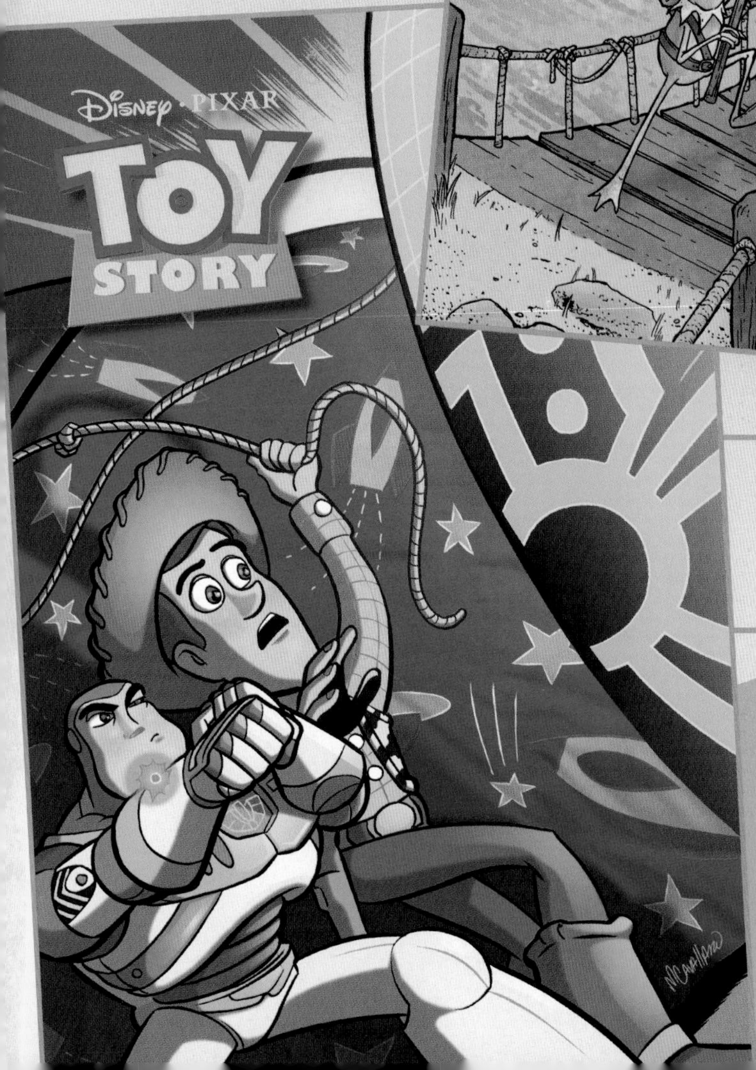
DISNEY · PIXAR
TOY
STORY

TOY STORY: MYSTERIOUS STRANGER

SC $9.99 ISBN 9781934506912
HC $24.99 ISBN 9781608865239

TOY STORY:
THE RETURN OF BUZZ LIGHTYEAR

SC $9.99 ISBN 9781608865574
HC $24.99 ISBN 9781608865581

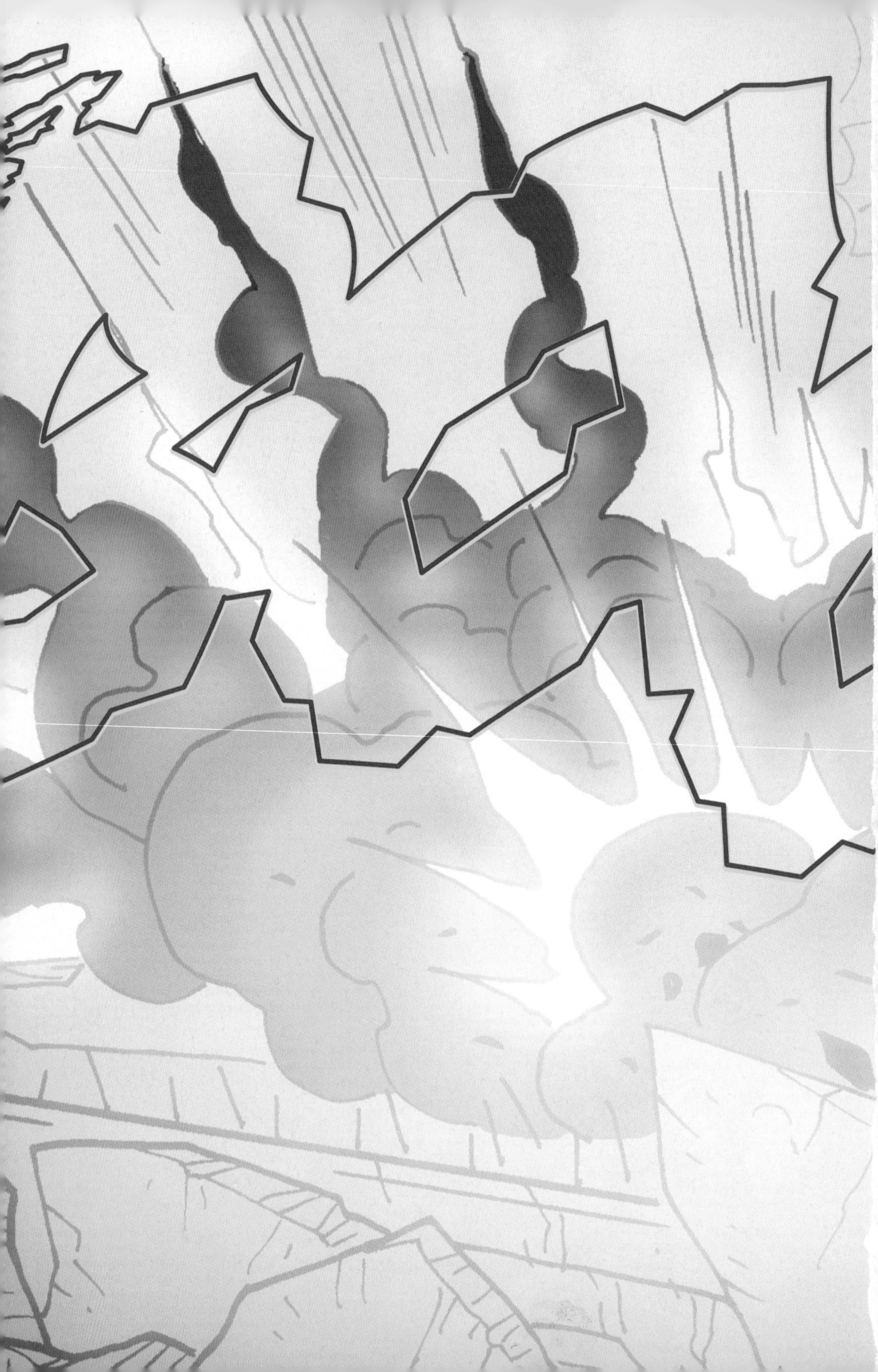

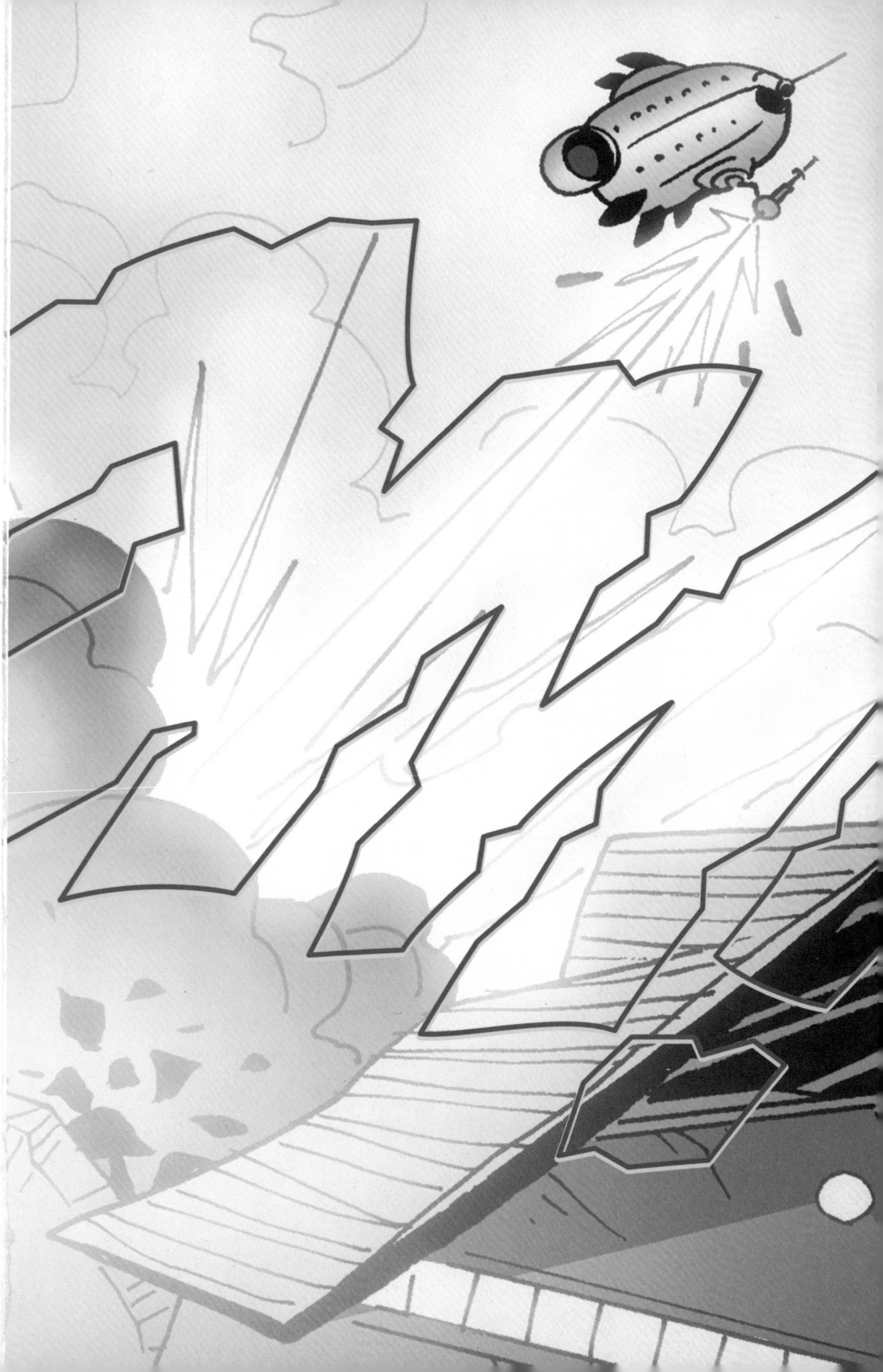